THE INVISIBLE KID
AND THE INTERGALACTIC RV

By Terry and Wayne Baltz

Red Feather Books

The Invisible Kid Series:

#1 *The Invisible Kid And Dr. Poof's Magic Soap*

#2 *The Invisible Kid And The Killer Cat*

#3 *The Invisible Kid And The Intergalactic RV*

Threshold Books

Night Of The Falling Stars

THE INVISIBLE KID AND THE INTERGALACTIC RV

by

Terry and Wayne Baltz

Cover Design & Illustration by Gary Raham

A Red Feather Book

PRAIRIE DIVIDE PRODUCTIONS
Fort Collins, Colorado

This is a work of fiction. The characters, incidents, and dialogues in this book are all products of the authors' rampant imaginations and are certainly not to be construed as real. Except, of course, while you are reading the book.

What *is* real, however, and what we hope you may find a glimpse of in this story, is the grandeur and the sheer immensity of the universe in which we live. Consider just this one amazing truth: If you wished to visit the nearby Andromeda Galaxy, and you could travel at the rather high rate of speed of 1,000 miles every second(!), it would take you *465 million years* to get there (without a wormhole).

Published by Prairie Divide Productions
305 W. Magnolia, Suite 116
Fort Collins, CO 80521

Back cover photo of the Great Galaxy in Andromeda: Palomar Obs./California Institute of Technology, by permission

Library of Congress Catalogue Card Number: 97-76601

Printed in the U.S.A.
Text printed on 100% recycled paper manufactured without the use of dioxin-producing elemental chlorine.

ISBN 1-884610-13-7

For Luz Lara,

man of light and mirrors

⇌ One ⇋

A week before Halloween I lost my best friends — my best *human* friends — Kathleen and Eddie. Not only that, but on that very same day Bumps — my best *dog* friend — began to get weird on me.

We were all in the cemetery, just a few blocks from my house. It's an old cemetery, and nobody keeps it up much anymore. The grass is thin and the tombstones are chipped and stained black with age. Some say the place is haunted, but I don't believe in that stuff.

We were collecting walnuts from our favorite black walnut tree at the top of the hill. The wind swirled red and orange leaves at our feet. Grey clouds hung heavy in the sky. It was Friday afternoon, late October, and the world was darkening toward winter.

Eddie took a stick and whacked a walnut hanging from a branch just over his head. "Did you see *The Black Hole Will Get You If You Don't Watch Out* last night, Casey?" he asked, scrunching his eyes shut as the black walnut clobbered him. "It was the best."

"Nope." I was really embarrassed that I'd missed that movie, so I covered as best I could. "I was busy," I said. I'd been busy sleeping.

"Busy?" Kathleen shot me a surprised look. "Busy doing what, Casey? Washing clothes? Dusting?"

"Just busy," I said. "If you must know, I was making plans for Halloween. It's only eight days from now."

Eddie had worked the husk off the walnut. He tossed it to me and began working on another. I cracked it open with a rock. We sat in the leaves, our backs against the tree, and shared the sweet pieces. The air turned sharply cold. I pulled my jacket hood over my head.

"Halloween," Kathleen whispered, as if savoring the sound. Then she jumped to her feet. "Let's have an old-fashioned Halloween this year," she announced. "You know, jack-o-lanterns, ghost stories."

"Witches, vampires, ghosts," Eddie said.

"None of this 'go as your favorite action hero' stuff." She snapped her fingers. "As a matter of fact, we could *all* be ghosts. Right, Casey?"

"I'm the only one who can really be a ghost," I said.

Kathleen's eyebrows rose to her hairline. "What do you mean by that, Cassandra Ann Granger?"

"I'm the one with the magic soap. So I can be the ghost that really *looks* like a ghost. You and Eddie would have to wear sheets. Kind of ridiculous." Somehow I had forgotten that I had worn a sheet myself just last Halloween. But that was before I found Dr. Poof's Magic Soap, the soap that makes me invisible.

"You wouldn't share?" Kathleen tapped her foot. "With your friends?" Up and down, up and down. She was getting annoyed.

"Yeah, we could all be ghosts," Eddie said. "Just picture us going house to house totally invisible. We'd say, 'Trick or treat' and they would only see our loot bags hanging in thin air. They'd probably faint! Cool!" He burst out laughing. Kathleen joined in and before you could say "Trick or treat" they were rolling down the hill. "Ghosts! Ghosts!" they yelled as they rolled through the leaves. Bumps ran alongside, barking at them.

"Well, forget it!" I called down to them. "I'm not going house to house this year. I'm throwing a party. The scariest, spookiest party you've ever seen. I'm going to scare you guys silly." What was I saying? Where was I going to have this scare-of-a-lifetime party? Not in my very unspooky, boring house. "And we can't all be ghosts," I added. "*I've* got the soap. *I'll* be the ghost. You two be something else."

Eddie and Kathleen sat up. They looked at each other, and even from the top of the hill I could see a spark pass between them. It was very disturbing. I decided to ignore it.

"Your house isn't scary, Casey," Kathleen said.

"I know that," I said. "I have another place in mind."

"Where?" Eddie asked.

Where? I wondered. "A different place," I said. "A perfect place."

"Come on, Casey, you're bluffing," Eddie said in his know-it-all way. "Let's go, Kathleen."

"What do you mean by that, Eddie?" I demanded.

"He means," answered Kathleen, "that you just made this idea up right now because you don't want to let us use your stupid soap to be invisible. You don't have any place in mind." She was tapping her foot hard. The ground rumbled.

"Just you wait, Kathleen," I said. What was I doing? Wait for what? Every time I opened my mouth I was getting myself into a bigger jam.

"Yeah, let's go, Eddie," Kathleen said. "I've got an idea." She started walking away.

"Kathleen, you never had an idea in your life," I said.

"Oh yeah, Casey? You have no idea what my idea is, and that's why you're mad."

"I don't care about your idea, Kathleen. I wouldn't waste my time thinking about your idea." She kept walking. "And I'm not mad!" I yelled, throwing a walnut husk at her back.

The wind whipped at her long brown hair. "Come on, Eddie. We have plans to make," she called, without even looking back.

Eddie started after her. Then he stopped and turned to me. "Casey, I think you've gone too far this time," he said.

I threw a husk after Eddie, too. Bumps dove at it, caught it up in his jaws and shook it as though it were a mouse. I threw a walnut down the hill to the edge of the woods. Bumps chased it, leaves launching themselves in whirlwinds behind him. I ran after him, the cold wind pushing me forward. I felt wild and free as I tugged the walnut out of Bumps' jaws and threw it deep into the woods. "We don't need them, do we, Bumps," I muttered. Bumps disappeared through the bushes and into the woods, swallowed up in a kaleidoscope of autumn color. I followed.

Deeper in the woods the trees crowded together. Daylight dimmed, replaced by a forbidding gloom. I called to Bumps. "We should be going home," I told him. But he only looked back, shook the walnut to remind me of our game, and disappeared down the darkening path, into a part of the woods I had never explored before. I ran after him, tripping over tree roots, branches slashing at me, leaves falling thick and fast.

The path ended in a small clearing. It was an unwelcoming place. Weathered gravestones poked through the ground like huge skeleton fingers. An ancient house squatted heavily just in front of the far trees. It was a wreck, battered by time and neglect. Rot had eaten holes in the walls, windows were shattered, shutters dangled and banged in the wind, a porch post lay dead on the steps. At one corner, a four-sided tower jutted skyward. It seemed almost alive, a menacing guard with a watchful eye, warding off all intruders.

Bumps sniffed around the porch steps for a few seconds, jerked back as if he'd been burned, and let out a horrible howl.

⇌ Two ⇋

Bumps wouldn't stop howling. Not after we got out of the woods — running full speed all the way — and not after we got home. He wasn't too popular with my family. Dad tried to coax him to stop with treats. No luck. Then he tried yelling, which only made Bumps howl louder. Mom put him outside. He barked. The neighbors complained. She let him back in. I cuddled and petted him and he finally settled into a steady whine.

Even after we got into bed and Bumps snuggled against my feet, he whined. I wondered what could have disturbed him so much at the old house. I was beginning to think of it as the old *haunted* house.

* * *

The next morning Bumps wouldn't touch his dog food. He looked up at me and barked as if he were trying to tell me something important. My snotty sister Penny said, "That dog's weird. Cute. But weird."

"Shut up, Penny. He's not weird."

"I remember when you brought him home last Halloween," Mom said.

"I didn't bring him home. After I got home he bumped at the door, that's all."

"Right," Penny said. "He walks into doors. Weird."

"Quit it," I said. "He understands everything you say." Bumps barked. "See?" I said.

"Weird dog. Weird sister," Penny said.

"That's enough, Penny," Mom said. "Don't you have any idea what's wrong with him, Casey?" she asked. "He's been upset since you got home yesterday."

I shrugged. I had an idea, but I wanted to keep the haunted house a secret for now. It had occurred to me that it just might be a great place for a really scary Halloween party. Who could top a setting like that? Halloween in a haunted house.

"Take him for a walk or something," Mom said. "Go see Terence and Sophie. I promised Sophie some of my basil in return for the peppermint she gave me." She thrust a bunch of sweet smelling dried herbs tied with a string into my hands. Bumps barked. "Go anyplace," Mom groaned, "but go now." She pushed me toward the door.

Bumps and I headed toward Uncle Terence O'Toole's Lucky Leprechaun Shoe Shop. Uncle Terence is really Kathleen's uncle but he's always felt like mine, too, so I call him uncle. I'm glad he lets me. I don't have any uncles of my own. Even though he's pretty old, Uncle Terence recently got married for the first time. To Sophie. I like Sophie now, but at first I didn't because I thought she had bewitched Uncle Terence and Kathleen. And she had, but only with her enchanting nature and good heart.

Due to Bumps' barking and the peculiar looks we were getting, I ran almost the whole mile to the shop. As we rounded the last corner I thought I saw Kathleen and Eddie at the door of the shop. I called out. It was them all right.

But instead of answering, they ran down the sidewalk, going the other way. Were they avoiding me?

"Welcome," Uncle Terence called over his shoulder as I let Bumps and myself into the shop. He was busy mending the sole of a big brown shoe. "What brings you to this part of the world?" Bumps ran up to him, yiping, and practically jumped onto his workbench. "But hold on. Something's wrong with the wee dog," Uncle Terence said. I nodded. "Take him up to Sophie, quick. She'll know what to do."

Their apartment above the shop always smells wonderful. Today it was the aroma of cinnamon. Sophie's huge black cat, Camomile, met us at the already open doorway. She rubbed herself against Bumps and purred. Bumps barked.

"What a lovely bunch of basil. Is that for me, Cassandra?" Sophie said, coming in from the kitchen with a plateful of cinnamon cookies.

"Sure is, Sophie. From my mom," I said taking one of the cookies she offered.

She broke one and offered a small piece each to Camomile and Bumps. Neither ate it. Sophie knelt in front of Bumps. "What's bothering you, Bumps?"

Bumps did what he'd been doing best — he barked. Sophie did what she does best — she listened.

After a few minutes Bumps stopped barking. "Okay," Sophie said softly, "okay, Bumps." She patted his head. Bumps flopped down as if he didn't have a care in the world. "I can't get all that he said, but part of it seems to be 'Space: The frontier is closer than we think.' Cassandra, have you been filling this dog's head with *Star Trip* movies late at night?"

Of course I had. That's what I always do. *Star Trip*, and *It Came From The Outer Limits*, and that black hole movie from the other night if I'd known about it. Bumps almost always watches them with me when I sneak downstairs late at night.

"I don't think that's it, Sophie," I said. "Those movies were days ago. Bumps just started up like this yesterday." At the haunted house, I thought. It had to be that house. As if it were haunting Bumps. Until now, that is. Now he was scrunched into Camomile's side, snoring softly. Cam purred.

"Did something happen to upset him yesterday?" Sophie asked.

"We were in the cemetery," I said. "Eddie and Kathleen and I had a fight. Maybe that upset him."

Sophie gave me a look, as though she suspected there was more than I was telling. "Well, whatever it was, at least he seems content now that he's delivered his message," she said.

I ate some more cookies and drank a big glass of milk while Bumps slept. Then I took Bumps home. He was sound asleep again on my bed before I closed the door. Space: The frontier is closer than we think? I wondered what that could mean. Well, whatever it meant would have to wait. I had plans to make, and one thing I was sure of: A haunted house is a good place for a Halloween party. I had to check that place out. But first I wanted to check on Kathleen and Eddie. What were they up to?

My first stop was Kathleen's house. I rang the bell and knocked. No one answered so I let myself in. That's the way we do it, Kathleen and I. I heard voices in the kitchen.

"Kathleen?" I called. The voices stopped. By the time I got to the kitchen, the back door was closing. I zoomed to the door. Kathleen and Eddie were racing around the corner of the house. They *were* avoiding me!

I got mad. Right then and there. Really mad. If that's the way they're going to treat me, then I'll avoid them too, I decided. They aren't going to get to me. I'll just scare them to death at my party.

As soon as I got home the phone rang. I wasn't going to talk to Kathleen or Eddie. Just in case it was one of them I answered in a high, squeaky voice, "Helloooo?"

"Casey?" It was Kathleen.

"There is no Casey here," I said, changing to a gruff, low voice.

"Casey, I know that's you," she said.

I tried high and squeaky again. "I am sorry, you have the wrong number," I said, and hung up.

Ring. Ring. Ring. Ring. . . .

I picked it up on the tenth ring. In my gruff voice I said, "Hello."

"Casey, you're not fooling anybody. I know it's you," Kathleen said.

"Wrong number," I said and pressed the hang-up button.

Ring.

I picked it up right away and said in my gruff voice, "If you don't stop playing with the phone, I'm going to —"

"You're going to what, Casey?" It was not Kathleen.

"Oh, it's you, Mom."

"Why were you talking like that? Has someone been —"

"No, Mom. Everything's fine. I just thought it was Kathleen."

"You talk to your best friend like that?"

"We were only joking around. How's work?" I asked, hoping to get her off the subject.

"Don't ask. That's why I called. Not only do I have to work on Saturday, but now it looks like I'll have to be here all day. Is your dad back from golf?"

"No."

"I didn't think so. Those games seem to take all weekend." Mom wasn't a fan of golf. "Penny home?"

"No."

"I guess she won't be back until late. It's that new boyfriend, Clark."

"Mark," I corrected.

"Really? I thought Mark was last year."

"You're thinking of Mark One," I said. "This is Mark Two."

"Oh." She sounded distracted. "Well, got to get back. Don't get into any trouble. Bye." *Click.*

That's when I made my plans.

⇌ Three ⇋

No one was home. I could do anything I wanted. I could use Dr. Poof's Magic Soap to become invisible. I could spy on Kathleen and Eddie. I could even check out that haunted house. All totally, completely invisible. This was going to be fun.

Bumps was still sleeping on the bed, so I tiptoed over to my secret hiding place — the old metal Band Aid box in my dresser drawer next to my comb and brush. But now the box only contained a slightly used bar of Dr. Poof's Magic Soap. "Well, here goes," I said to myself in the mirror.

I washed my clothes and canvas shoes in the washer with a sliver of the soap and washed myself in the shower with the rest. While I waited to disappear I dried my clothes in the dryer. About twenty minutes later my clothes and I faded away. Putting invisible clothes on an invisible body has always been difficult for me. Sometimes I come back visible with my shirt on backwards.

I didn't know how long I would stay invisible. I *did* know my mom and dad wouldn't like an invisible kid eating dinner with them. Too weird. They might call out the National Guard, or at least the local police. I also knew, from experience, that being invisible isn't as easy as it looks. But I had my plan:

1) Spy on Kathleen and Eddie.

2) Check out the haunted house.
3) Ask Kathleen to let me stay over at her house tonight.

She'd let me stay over invisible before. She'd snuck food up to her bedroom and let me sleep on her twin bed. That was the plan. A good plan, I thought. So how did everything go so wrong?

Finding Kathleen and Eddie wasn't the hard part. Eddie's bicycle was parked right outside Kathleen's house. The front door was locked, so I rang the doorbell. Mrs. O'Toole answered on the second ring. "Hello?" she said, looking surprised because no one was there. She stepped out onto the porch, holding the door open with one hand as she looked up and down the sidewalk. I ducked inside and began my search.

They were easy to find. Muffled laughter was coming from the basement, from the room that used to be Uncle Terence's work room. It had become the family room since Uncle Terence moved to The Lucky Leprechaun Shoe Shop.

I tiptoed down a few steps. Eddie and Kathleen sat on the couch near the bottom of the stairs. But I could only hear Eddie say ". . . Halloween . . ." and Kathleen say ". . . Casey . . ." so I tiptoed down a few more. Suddenly Kathleen dropped her voice to a whisper and I couldn't understand anything! Then, just as suddenly, she said in a louder-than-normal voice, "How about another hand of cards, Eddie?" She picked a deck of cards off the coffee table and shuffled them clumsily.

"I hate cards," Eddie said. Kathleen shot him one of her killer looks. "Oh, right. Let's play solitaire," he said. "I'll beat you this time." Solitaire? I'll beat you this time? Was Eddie nuts? Kathleen shot him another look. "I mean poker," he said. "Let's play another hand of poker." Kathleen killed him again. "What's wrong *now*?" he asked.

Kathleen doesn't know how to play poker. I know that for a fact. That's what was wrong. Kathleen laughed in this fake genteel lady sort of way. "Oh, Eddie," she said. "Joker! What a poker you are. I mean, poker! What a joker you are."

That broke Eddie up until Kathleen stomped on his foot. He gasped, looked perplexed and then pulled himself together, snapped his fingers and said, "Old maid. Let's play old maid again."

That convinced me. Somehow they knew I was there. "How'd you know I was here?" I asked.

Kathleen jumped. "Casey, you scared me."

"No, I didn't. You knew I was here. All that lame talk about solitaire and poker and old maid."

"Yeah, but you still scared me."

"What are you guys up to?" I said.

"None of your business," Kathleen said.

"Well then, at least tell me how you knew I was here." I was begging. I hate it when I beg, but I had to know.

"I heard you," she said. "Invisible people still make noise, you know. That one step creaks. Besides, Casey, you've always had trouble being quiet."

"And I could smell you," Eddie said.

"Not that again, Eddie," I said.

"The burning smell from the soap," he said scrunching his nose. "Remember?"

I'd forgotten that using the soap leaves an odor behind. And I'd forgotten about Eddie's extraordinary sense of smell. Or maybe it isn't so extraordinary. Maybe he just pays more attention than most people do.

"So what's up?" I said.

"We were planning a Halloween treat for you," Kathleen said. Eddie laughed evilly. Kathleen jabbed him with her pointy elbow. "Don't spoil it by asking," she said. "Anyway, what's the idea of spying on us? It's not fair," she whined.

"It's not fair," I said, imitating her whine. "Oh, by the way, I have to stay over at your house until I get visible again which will probably be tomor —"

"No," she said.

"No?"

"N-O. No." I could see that begging wouldn't help.

"That's okay," I said, as though it didn't matter in the least. "I have a better idea anyway. And some very important things to do before my Halloween party."

"We're looking forward to that," Eddie said.

What does he mean by that? I wondered, as I tiptoed back up the stairs. But I had a more immediate problem since Kathleen wouldn't let me stay over: Where to hide out until I was visible again.

The only answer was Uncle Terence and Sophie's. They're the only other people who have "seen" me invisible before. So they're the only ones who wouldn't call the police. Another good reason to go to Sophie and Uncle Terence's was that I'd missed lunch and now it was nearly supper time. And Sophie makes the best food. She uses lots of herbs and spices. Maybe she was making spaghetti sauce with the basil I'd brought over. I could almost taste the sauce as I let myself in the back door and climbed the steps to their apartment.

"Can you see who that is, darlin'?" said Uncle Terence from the back somewhere.

Sophie came out. "I think it must be Cassandra, because I don't see anyone."

"Hi, Sophie," I said.

"Is she up to her old tricks again?" Uncle Terence said.

"Seems so," Sophie said. "Come in, Cassandra. Sit on the sofa there so we know where you are. Who are you spying on today?" Uncle Terence came in. "Don't sit on her, dear. She's over there on the sofa. I just asked her who she's spying on this time."

Uncle Terence leaned against the door frame and looked a little to the left of me as he talked. "Good question. Nosey, though, this spying business. Don't you think, Casey? Reminds me a wee bit of Eddie Maskit, it does."

"It does not. Not at all," I said with feeling. "Eddie's just a double pain in the . . ."

"Okay, dear, we get the point," Sophie said, looking me right in the eye. How does she do that? I wondered.

"I was spying on Kathleen and Eddie," I said, "and now Kathleen won't let me stay over until I get visible again. Can I stay here?"

"Sure," Uncle Terence said, "except we're going out to dinner at my brother's." His brother is Kathleen's dad. They were going to Kathleen's house, of all places. "So you'll be alone for awhile," he said.

"That's okay."

"And we don't have any real supper to feed you."

That wasn't okay. I was starved.

Sophie said. "Call your mom and dad, Cassandra, so they'll know where you are."

I went into the study and called home. Dad answered. "Hi Dad," I said.

"Casey, there's no food in the house. When's your mother coming home?"

"She had to work all day today and I'm staying over at Uncle Terence and Sophie's."

"In that case I'll take your mother out to dinner. Have fun and give my best to Terence and Sophie." Great. Everybody eats but me.

Sophie was in the kitchen. On the table — I couldn't believe it! — was some very basilly-smelling spaghetti. "Leftovers from lunch," she said scooping huge amounts onto a plate. "Your mother's basil was perfect." She smiled at me as I forked spaghetti into my invisible mouth.

After I finished eating I was just sitting quietly in a chair, when Uncle Terence came into the room and patted me on the head. Before I even got a chance to ask him how he knew where I was, he said, "Not much use being invisible if you're going to put spaghetti sauce on your face."

Kathleen heard me on the stairs. Eddie smelled me. And I always get spaghetti sauce on my face. It isn't easy being an invisible kid.

And, already, parts one and three of my plan had failed: spying on Eddie and Kathleen, and staying over at Kathleen's house. But I wasn't going to give up. It was time to work on the other part of the plan — checking out that haunted house. Finally, when Uncle Terence and Sophie left, that's just what I did.

Camomile followed me down the stairs and slipped out the back door with me. A mouse darted between the trash cans. "Go get him, Cam," I urged. But she stuck to me like a shadow, like a rat to cheese, like a nut to a bolt, like a sitter to a baby. "Did Sophie tell you to stay with me while they're gone?" I asked her. Camomile, my shadow, followed me down streets, past my house and into the old cemetery.

The air was sharp and clear, but it was dark now, and once we started down the path into the woods it grew darker still. Cam had no trouble finding her way, just as she never had any trouble knowing where I was, invisible or not. But I couldn't even see the path in front of me. *I* was the shadow now, tripping along behind Cam. We finally reached the clearing and the massive old house, silent and dark, with barely a glint of starlight in its many windows. Definitely an eerie place. And though I knew better than to really believe it was "haunted," I figured it would be enough to scare the pants off Kathleen and Eddie.

At that very moment a weird greenish light flickered in the windows of the tower.

⇌ Four ⇋

Within seconds a shimmering green light played around the tower windows and seeped out of every pore of the battered old house. I was all for getting out of there, and getting out quick.

"Cam," I squeaked, "Let's go." But she ignored me. In fact, she jumped onto the porch and walked right up to a hole in the door made by a broken board. Green light oozed out of it, but Cam didn't hesitate. She squeezed through, and she was gone.

I don't know how much time went by while I tried to find the courage to go after her. I thought about all the horrible things that could have happened to her. I thought even more about all the horrible things that might happen to *me* if I followed. But I couldn't lose that cat. She was getting to be a good friend, and Sophie was a good friend already. After what seemed like years I finally got the nerve. I climbed the steps to the porch.

The door was unlocked, and opened with a definite haunted house *creak* when I barely touched it. I jumped. The hall was dark except for the green light flowing down a staircase. Camomile was nearing the top of those stairs.

"Come back, Cam," I whispered, and my whisper sounded like a loudspeaker in that tomb.

Cam paid no attention. She vanished into the green light at the top of the stairs. A second later a door slammed somewhere up there and the light dimmed. I groped my way up the steps, sliding my hands along a rickety wooden railing and wiping cobwebs from my face.

Four closed doors waited for me in the upstairs hall. Green light streamed out from under only one, the door at the end of the hall. Even though there was no doubt in my mind that that was the door that had closed behind Camomile — or maybe *because* there was no doubt — I opened all the other doors looking for her. Empty rooms, every one.

I forced my feet to take me to the door at the end of the hall. I willed my hand around the doorknob. Then I was stuck. I couldn't get my body to do any more. Not until I heard Cam's *meow* behind that door. A plaintive *meow*. Without thinking, I turned the knob and pushed. The door flew open.

This room was empty, too, except for one important difference: A dark, narrow, spiral staircase wound upward — to the tower room, I realized. Green light poured like a waterfall down that stairs, bathing Cam who stood like a statue just five steps up. I climbed the ancient, winding steps toward Cam.

Suddenly the green light disappeared, and Cam and I were wrapped in darkness. Then the door opened above us. I held my breath. To my surprise, a boy about my age appeared at the top of the stairs. He was holding a candle. I didn't recognize him from the neighborhood, but I knew I was safe no matter who it was because I was invisible. Except, I suddenly realized, I'm standing directly in his path if he comes down the stairs. Cam broke her pose and started up the stairs toward the stranger. I was about to follow when the boy looked right at Cam and said, "Greetings, Earthling." I wanted to laugh, but I kept quiet. Cam stopped in her tracks and meowed a friendly meow. "Who's that with you?" the boy asked. More meows from Cam. "Really?" the boy said. "A human being? Not at all what they look like in the travel brochures and movies. Greetings, other Earthling," he said, and this time he looked right at me. As if I were visible. I looked at myself. I wasn't.

He was about my height, maybe half an inch shorter, probably eleven or twelve. "Greetings, Earthlings," he said again. His hair was the color of honey, and he had wide-set grey eyes. What was he doing here at this time of night, and why was he looking at me as if he could see me? He looked puzzled. "Isn't that the proper greeting on this planet?"

He wore a shimmering green and silver shirt and pants and silver shoes. This planet? Strange kid, I thought. "You're a week early for Halloween," I said.

"You don't look as substantial as the human beings shown on your television. Or even as this small feline. She is a feline, is she not?" Cam was rubbing against the boy's leg and purring.

"Don't be silly. She's a cat. A *big* cat. Who are you? What are you doing here? And what was that green light?"

But he wasn't listening. "I know what it is," he blurted. "I'm not seeing you in the visible light spectrum. I'm seeing you in infrared."

"Infra who?" I asked.

"I'm seeing the electromagnetic radiation of your body. The part outside of your visible spectrum, below red. But why would that be?" He seemed to be asking himself. And even though I didn't know what he was talking about, I was pretty sure I knew the answer.

"Because I'm invisible."

"But you're not. I can see your infrared radiation."

"Well, then I guess I'm not invisible to you. But to most people I am. How can you see this what-do-you-call-it red?"

"The travel guides do not mention invisible humans. How did you get this way? Are you diseased?" he asked instead of answering my question.

"No. I have this soap and . . . Wait a minute. Who are you? Where are you from? What did you mean, 'this planet'? What are you doing in here? And what was that green light?"

"To answer your questions in reverse order: The green light powers this spaceship, the control room is up there." He gestured toward the tower room. "I'm here on vacation. I wanted to know if 'Greetings, Earthling' is the correct form of introduction on this planet. I am from a nearby galaxy many trillions of miles from here. My name is not translatable into your language because we have 132 letters in our alphabet and you only have 26. I'm just an old retired man who needed a break from his family. I have children, and grandchildren, and great grandchildren."

Okay, he was pretty good at fast answers, but they were completely ridiculous ones. And still more questions piled up in my head. "What do you mean 'grandchildren'?" I scoffed. "You're only my age."

"Oh no, much older." He laughed and his laughter was like bells ringing out from far away across a field. "You see, there's some kind of a glitch in this model RV, or recreational vehicle, I'm using. When I go through a wormhole and come out in another part of the universe, my physical body goes back in time. This is how I used to look many, many years ago. It's rather a lot of fun. This transformation will persist until I return through the wormhole to my space habitat in my own galaxy."

This was too much.

"Please, come up to the control room," he said. "It's really where I live. The rest of the place is pretty spooky, yes?" He held the candle out to light the spiral staircase and he went up. Cam followed, so I did, too. Amazingly, the tower room *did* look like a spacecraft. The walls were crammed with dials and meters and switches. A soft white light came from every direction, even the ceiling and the floor, and seemed to create warmth as well as light. I was beginning to get just a little bit curious!

"What galaxy are you from?" I asked.

"Come to the window," he said. The light in the room went out as if by magic, and stars popped out in the sky. He pointed. "Andromeda," he said. "On a clear night like this you can just barely see it."

I looked where he was pointing. "I don't see anything," I said. "Just a little whiff of cloud."

He smiled. "That's not a cloud. Not like you mean, anyway. It's a cloud of *stars*. More than a hundred billion suns. My planet orbits one of them."

"A hundred billion?" I said. "That's pretty big, isn't it?"

"Precisely," he said. "Much like your own galaxy."

"Wait a minute. First you said it was nearby and trillions of miles from here. That doesn't make any sense. And now you say it's big, but how come it looks so small?" I challenged.

"Close is a relative term. Andromeda *is* close, astronomically speaking: only about two and a half million light-years. A light-year is the distance that light travels in a year, which is almost six trillion miles. So two and a half million light-years is about fifteen million trillion miles. That's a '15' with 18 zeroes after it. But there are objects in the universe thousands of times farther away. So, you see, Andromeda is both close *and* very far away."

"Oh my liver," I said. Then I decided to put him on the spot. "So tell me about wormholes," I said. "What do you know about wormholes?"

"Quite a bit," he said proudly. "You see, even traveling at the speed of light — which we have found to be quite impossible, I might add — it would take two and a half million years to get here from Andromeda. Of course, that's too long. That's why I came by wormhole. It's a shortcut, a hole in space-time."

"I don't get it," I said. Maybe it was *me* on the spot.

"Imagine this," he said. "An ant is walking on a very large piece of paper, let's say one the size of the United States. And let's say this little ant is in the middle of the paper, and is trying to get to a place exactly on the opposite side, the underside."

"That would be a long walk," I said.

"Yes. But what if the ant found a hole in the paper?"

"It could go through," I said. "It wouldn't be far at all."

"A wormhole is like that," he said, "only faster."

"How long does it take?"

"Less time than it takes to blink your ear."

"You mean my eye, don't you?"

"Precisely. Blink your eye."

"That's fast." He nodded. "So you're going home by a wormhole, too, I suppose."

"That's my plan," he said quietly, and he just kept looking up at the beautiful black sky. "Come and sit down," he said finally. Reclining chairs blossomed from the floor in front of a softly glowing control panel. "Although it was not part of my plan, I am truly honored to have a cat and a human visiting. What are your names, so I may call you properly?"

I told him mine, and just as I started to tell him Cam's she meowed. "Camomile," he said. "Hmm. Isn't that the name of a herbal beverage? Which reminds me to ask, what would you like to eat and drink?" Cam meowed again. "Tuna," he said and touched a control. A bowl popped out of the panel and with it the unmistakable smell of tuna. Cam attacked it as if it were alive and ate it all. "And you, Casey?"

Cam seemed all right so I asked for popcorn, my favorite before-bed snack. A bowl of popcorn popped out of the panel. It was yummy. "What about that green light? What was that for?" I asked between bites.

"I was synchronizing the peripheral dopulator production system. If I don't do it every few Earth hours the central prodibulator induction valve could become . . . destructed. . . . Maybe."

I nodded as though I knew just what he was talking about. "Run that last part by me again, will you?" I said.

"The central prodibulator induction valve could become . . . become . . ." He scratched his head. "I don't think destructed is quite the proper word. Could it become *in*structed?" He was asking me!

"I don't think so," I said. "How about *con*structed?"

"No, that's not it."

"*Ob*structed?" I said.

"Precisely!" He smiled happily.

"Good," I smiled back. "What are you talking about, though?"

He looked down and scuffed one shoe across the toe of the other. He scratched his head again. Finally he said, "I don't think I can put it any more simply."

"Well, what would happen if the ibulator valve thing *did* become obstructed?"

"No go," he said.

"Gotcha." I finished off the last of the popcorn. "Why are you telling me all this? Aren't you afraid I'll tell about you and then the townspeople will come to get you like in *Edward Clipperfingers*?"

"Not really. Who believes a child, or even an adult, when they tell about something above the usual? Remember *The Day Everything On Earth Stopped Working*?"

"True," I said. I was beginning to like this kid a little. "How do you know these movies?" I asked. "Not being from Earth and all, I mean." Maybe I was even beginning to *believe* him.

"When the wormhole's just right we get your television transmissions. I like Earthmade movies," he said. "It's getting late. Do you live near here?"

"Yeah. A few blocks. But I'm staying at my friends' house tonight. See, since I'm invisible — well, sort of invisible — I can't go home."

"Your parents don't like you this way?" he asked.

"My parents don't even know I *am* this way; and if they did, they wouldn't like it, no." He flicked a switch and a section of the wall became a map of St. Louis. "What's this?" I said.

"This is your way home tonight," he said. "Can you point to where your friends live?"

After some searching I found the street that The Lucky Leprechaun Shoe Shop is on. "Along here somewhere," I said.

"Touch the screen where you think it is," he instructed. I touched the screen. Immediately the map changed, showing now just the area around where I had touched, but magnified to fill the whole screen. The image was more like an aerial photograph now. It showed not only the street arrangement but the buildings and trees. "Good," he said. "Now, can you show me more precisely the location of their domicile?"

"I don't even know if they have one. You still want to know where they live?" I asked.

"Precisely."

I studied the new map. "Probably this building here," I said. "I'm not quite sure. This is close, though." He motioned for me to touch the screen again. I did. A new picture appeared. It was as if a photograph had been taken from the middle of the street just a short distance from The Lucky Leprechaun. More than that, it was as if I were standing in the middle of the street. For when I turned my head to the right or left the scene shifted to include the sights that would be visible to me were I actually there!

"Very good again," he said. "Now if you will just select the proper building —" Before he could finish I had poked my finger on the front door of Uncle Terence's shop. Just as I suspected it would, the picture changed to show the interior floor plan of the building. The basement, first floor, and second floor appeared side by side, showing doors and windows, stairways, even furniture. "And which is the bed you are sleeping in?" he asked.

"This one here," I said. "I always sleep there when I visit overnight with Uncle Terence and Sophie." I touched the screen but nothing happened. "What's the matter?" I asked.

"Hmm? Oh, nothing. Everything is functioning properly. Now, I want to explain this next part to you ahead of time. After I press this button here," he pointed to what looked like an elevator floor-selector that glowed dull orange, "the rules of the game will change such that within a nano-instant after your next touch on the screen you will find yourself in the place you have touched."

"You mean, if you press that button and I touch the bedroom here I'll *be* in the bedroom?"

"Yes. And, more precisely, you will be in the exact place you touch. It's best to be fairly careful."

"So this is like *Star Trip*, right? And this is a transporter unit."

"Well, in effect, but not in function. As I recall, the transporter units used by The Exitprise were based on a theory that matter can be disassembled into subatomic units, converted into electromagnetic energy patterns, transmitted across space to another location, and then reassembled."

I nodded. I was pretty sure it was something like that.

"That doesn't work," he said. "We tried it some centuries ago."

"I didn't think it would," I murmured. "*Star Trip* is just a story."

"It's based on two misconceptions. First, that we are somehow outside the universe and can manipulate it at will. Second, that things are merely a sum of their parts. At any rate, this transport system works on the principle that time and space are illusions. They do not really exist as we perceive them. In short, while we stand here talking, you also exist in the bed in question."

"You mean I'm already in bed?" I blurted.

"Precisely. More than that, you are always in bed. And you are always out of bed. You are always everywhere, because there is only one place and one time. Do you see?"

"No. How can I always be everywhere? There's only one of me."

"Well, yes, although numbers introduce another confusion. You see, numbers are only a tool. It's perfectly necessary to use them, so that we can function, but they don't make the illusions any more real."

My head was swimming. "So what actually happens if you push the button and I touch the screen here?" I said.

"The transporter mechanism emits an energy pulse which softens the quantum structure of this reality. When you touch the screen the subatomic particles simply realign themselves to reflect the alternate reality of your body in the place you have touched."

"I get transported?"

"Precisely."

"You don't expect me to believe any of this, do you?"

"Not really." He pressed the orange button. "Are you ready to go to bed?"

I wasn't sure. "Will it hurt?" I asked.

"Not a bit. You're already there, remember?"

I grabbed Cam in one arm and approached the wall with a shaky finger, holding it about an inch off the screen. "You really *aren't* from around here, are you?"

"Precisely."

I took a deep breath. I said, "Goodnight." Then I placed my finger right in the center of the queen-size bed in my uncle's spare room.

⇌ Five ⇋

Cam and I were lying comfortably in the center of the big bed in Uncle Terence's spare room. "Bull's eye!" I said, and fell asleep.

* * *

When I woke up it was bright morning, nearly 10 o'clock. I was back to normal, visible spectrum-wise. It wore off sooner than I would have expected. My body must be getting used to the effect of the soap. Or maybe the soap was getting weaker. Still, it was a good thing, being visible. I didn't need any more complications in my life right now.

Sophie and Uncle Terence met me in the kitchen with a cheery "Good morning" and an eager look in their eyes. Sophie got right to the point. "I heard you and Camomile had quite an interesting evening, Cassandra."

Camomile sat nearby, innocently licking her paw. "We did," I admitted.

"Care to tell us about it?" Uncle Terence asked, his eyes glowing with curiosity.

I was unsure about how much I wanted to share and I wondered how much Sophie had gotten from Cam. "Not now," I said. "I'm not ready yet."

"Cam gives me the clear message that there is no danger for you with this . . . person. What do *you* think?" Sophie asked.

"He's all right," I said.

"Okay, then," Sophie said. Cam meowed. "And she says she'd like to go with you again next time."

* * *

Later that day I was off with Cam to the haunted house. On the way over I thought I saw Eddie and Kathleen sneaking around, but I didn't care what they were up to. I had my own adventure.

As the old house came into view through the trees, I began to doubt my whole experience last night. "How can someone be here from trillions of miles away?" I asked Camomile. "Why would he come here in a ship that looks like a haunted house?"

"Meow," said Cam just before she disappeared through the hole in the door.

I creaked the door open. Cam was already out of sight. The afternoon sun came through the windows at a low angle, lighting up cobwebs and dust floating in the air. Clouds that had been building in the west blotted out the sun. A low moan echoed through the house, sending shivers up my spine.

"Hello?" I called in a shriveled voice. The house moaned some more. "Help?" I whispered, backing toward the door.

"Casey!" The strange visitor from another galaxy was standing at the top of the stairs, Cam wrapping herself around his ankles. "You look wonderful all visible. Come up."

I took the steps two at a time. "Is this place haunted?" I asked as I reached the top.

"If you are referring to that low, modulated sound, I believe that's the sound the wind makes blowing through the broken windows," he said. "It is quite windy. A rainstorm is approaching."

"Is that all?" I said doubtfully. Thunder boomed in the distance as if in answer.

"Don't be concerned, Casey. This isn't a haunted house. I told you: It's a spaceship. Come up and see my morning's work."

He climbed the stairs. He looked my age, but he moved more like my grandparents. "Why does it look like a haunted house then?" I asked.

"Simple," he said. "People like me, who come to Earth on vacation, want to be left alone. So one of the most requested RV models is the haunted house design. The theory is that Earthlings will avoid it. Apparently you, and Camomile, are not typical Earthlings." Again, the house moaned. It reminded me of that movie, *Valley Ghouls*. "But it's not really haunted," he said. "Not that I haven't heard of ghosts."

"Have you seen *Jasper, The Neighborly Ghost*?"

"No, but I enjoyed *The Ghost and Mrs. Moore.*" One of the bedroom doors was open at the top of the stairs. "Here we are," he said, and led me inside. He pointed proudly to a pile of multicolored leaves on the floor. "Your world is so very beautiful, with a tremendous variety of everything. The leaves here, for example, and more kinds of insects than sands on the beach, seasons — even the people, with their different levels of melanin providing varieties of skin color. Definitely an interesting planet to visit."

Camomile was busy nosing in the leaves. "What's the planet like that you come from?" I asked.

Rain burst from the clouds and pounded on the windows. He sat cross-legged on the floor. I did, too, and Cam curled in my lap. As he spoke he wove his hands gently through the leaves. "I can't say the actual name of my planet in English, but the meaning is the same as your word 'Earth'."

"You call your planet Earth?"

"Oh, yes, of course. Every world is called Earth by its people. In their own language, of course. It means 'the world on which we live'."

"What's it like on your Earth?"

"Actually we haven't lived there for over two hundred years. We live on a space habitat that orbits it."

"Why don't you live there?"

"We used up the natural resources at an alarming rate and polluted everything else. It's very desolate, although it is beginning to recover slowly. Someday we will be able to return, and if we've learned any lessons we'll live wiser next time."

"When will you be able to go back?"

"Not in my lifetime, nor in my grandchildren's. It was so beautiful, filled with a great variety of vegetation and animals. Our Earth was similar to yours — although our sky is pink, and we have three moons. There are very few planets as wonderful."

"Is that why you came here for a vacation?"

He nodded. "This vacation is very special to me. The cost of renting an RV and using the wormhole is very high. Not many can afford it. But before I retired, my work was Wormhole Security. Something like highway patrol here. So I got a substantial discount and here I am, ready to enjoy it all.

"Too bad it's raining."

"Not at all. I'm looking forward to going out in it. We don't have rain where I live. The habitat's kind of sterile, actually."

"How long will you be here?"

"The wormhole should maintain its current position for a few more weeks, but I will take a reading in a few days to check that. I must leave before the position changes, or I will have to wait for the wormhole's next run by."

"When will that be?" I asked.

"Wormholes are unpredictable. Could be a few years or a few millennia."

"What's a millennia?"

"A millenni*um* is a thousand years. Millennia is more than one millennium. And, as much as I like your planet, I would miss my friends and family. That's why I take readings on the wormhole. And that's why I synchronize the PDP system so often."

"PDP?"

"Peripheral dopulator production system. I told you before."

"Oh yeah. I couldn't forget that," I joked.

"Nor can I," he said. Only he wasn't joking. "I must be careful not to miss my chance."

⇌ Six ⇋

I was all alone in the house Sunday night, the night of the storm. Everyone was out, even Bumps, who had insisted on going out into the back yard in the rain and wind, against my advice. The real reason I wanted Bumps inside was — I didn't want to be alone. I felt jumpy and a little unreal since finding the haunted house RV.

A branch of our old oak wouldn't give up battering my bedroom window so I went downstairs, checking along the way to make sure that all the windows were closed. Just as I entered the kitchen the back door blew open. I hadn't latched it completely when I let Bumps out, I told myself. I called for Bumps. He didn't come, so I closed the door and locked it. I wondered if I had forgotten to lock the front door, too. It seemed like there were strange sounds in the house. Was that a creak of the hall floor? Then the phone rang, right next to me. I jumped a foot, then answered before it could make that horrible sound again.

"Hello!" I shouted. I was all nerves.

"Hi, Casey." It was Eddie. What does *he* want? I wondered.

"What do you want, Eddie?

"Uh . . . uh . . ." he said.

"Is that right? Anything else?"

"Uh . . . uh . . ." he repeated. I hung up.

Ring. I jumped again and grabbed that awful sounding phone.

"What, Eddie? What do you want? I have some very important things to do, so hurry up."

"Uh . . ."

"You told me about that last time, Eddie. Get on with it."

"What time is it, Casey? I just wanted to know what time it is."

"What *time* is it?" This was strange behavior, even for Eddie. "What's wrong, Eddie?" I said.

"What?" he asked. "Nothing," he answered hesitantly.

"I'm going now, Eddie." I slammed down thc receiver. That will teach him.

I thought I heard that noise again. It was the stairs now, *creak*, *creak*, *creaking*, like when I sneak down at midnight to watch a movie. I wasn't alone in the house. Or maybe I was imagining things.

A *bump* at the back door let me know that Bumps was ready to come in. I was never so glad to see him. I scooped the wet mess of dog into my arms and held him close. My shirt was getting sopping wet.

But suddenly Bumps got all wiggly and jumped down. His toenails clicked on the tile as he ran into the hall, his little tail wagging happily. A scream echoed through the house. It sounded like Kathleen's scream.

Kathleen stood in the hall, screaming as if it were a cobra instead of Bumps leaning against her leg. When she saw me she screamed again.

"Hold it, hold it," I said. "I'm the one who ought to be screaming, not you. This is *my* house you're sneaking around in, you know."

She caught her breath and hiccupped. "I was looking for . . . for you," she said. She sounded as guilty as if she'd said she was looking for priceless art objects to steal.

"Well? You found me. What do you want?" I wasn't too friendly. She had scared me, creaking around here.

"Uh . . . uh . . ." she said. Oh, no. The Eddie Syndrome strikes again.

"What?" I shouted. "What?"

Kathleen fiddled with a button on her blouse. She said, "My mother asked me to . . . to borrow coffee. We're out."

"This late at night?"

"She wanted to stay awake." Kathleen laughed suddenly, a little hysterically. "You know mothers." She shrugged.

I got Kathleen the coffee and she scurried out the door. Mr. Bumps wagged his tail as he watched her go. "Bumps, something doesn't feel right. I just don't believe all that about coffee. Maybe she was spying on me, like I was spying on her yesterday. I could call her mother and ask her if she's out of coffee, but then she would tell Kathleen. And then Kathleen would know I know something sneaky is going on." Bumps was listening to every word. I went on. "First, Eddie called for nothing, then Kathleen's sneaking around my house. Hmm. Seems to me that something's rotten in the state of . . . Where was it rotten, Bumps? Denver? No, that's not a state . . ." Bumps tilted his head. "Something's rotten in the state of Missouri," I said.

Suddenly the front door opened, and *both* Bumps and I jumped. It was my mom and dad, back from their evening out. "I'm never going to get to sleep tonight, not after all the coffee I had at the O'Toole's," my dad said.

"You were at Kathleen's house?" I asked. "I thought you went to a movie."

"We stopped in after," Mom said.

"Did Mrs. O'Toole send Kathleen over for coffee?" I asked.

"I don't know why she would. She had plenty."

I was right. Something *was* rotten in the state of Missouri.

The next morning before school I went to see my new and only friend. But he wasn't at the haunted house. In fact, the whole tower was *gone*.

⇌ Seven ⇋

I could hardly wait until school was over on Monday. I wanted to get back to the haunted house. I wanted to find out what had happened to the tower room. I wanted to ask my new friend a lot of questions about his galaxy and space travel. And also, I was feeling lonely. Eddie was keeping his distance, which was unusual since he'd been pestering me since kindergarten. And Kathleen goes to private school so I hadn't seen her since last night, and that was under peculiar and suspicious circumstances.

One thing I did find interesting at school was what we learned about Halloween that day. Halloween was actually New Year's Eve for the Celts. They lived a long time ago in Great Britain and northern France. Halloween marked the end of what they called the season of the sun, the growing season, and the beginning of the cold and dark season. They celebrated by eating a lot of food — food that they had grown during the summer. They lit bonfires in tribute to the dimming sunlight, and prepared for the long, cold sleep of nature. The Celts believed Halloween was the day that the walls between worlds were thinnest, and contact with one's ancestors could take place.

Of course, our Halloween was coming up in a few days, and I was getting worried. I didn't have a plan perfected for giving Eddie and Kathleen a good scare. I didn't even know if I could use the haunted house since it wasn't really a haunted house at all, but a spaceship that belonged to somebody else.

I found the tower room back where it belonged, and my friend inside it. He told me that he had taken a short trip in the tower — which is a space shuttle as well as the control room for the entire RV. He had gone to the Atlantic Ocean. "Tomorrow I plan on visiting the Arctic Circle," he said.

"Friday," I said. "Can I take a trip with you Friday after school?"

"Perhaps."

"But I have to get back before Saturday. Saturday is my Halloween party and there are these two friends of mine. They used to be friends of mine." Then, without my even expecting it, the whole story of our fight and everything that happened since then poured out.

"Maintaining friendships is both challenging and rewarding," he said. "We all make mistakes sometimes."

"Even people like you?"

"Like me? What do you mean?"

"You know, I thought space travelers were beyond fighting and all that."

"Where would you get that idea?" he said.

"I don't know. Movies?"

"Oh, I'm sure. Beyond-fighting movies like *War Of The Planets*, and *Freedom Day*, and *Foreigner*, and *Foreigners*, and *Foreigners 3*, and —"

"I just thought, you're so advanced and —"

"Rubbage!" he said.

"Rubbage? Do you mean garbage? Or rubbish?"

"Rubbish! Yes, precisely. Just because we found out how to use wormholes before you did doesn't mean that we are more advanced in *every* way. Look at what we did to our planet! The most important advances are in wisdom and compassion, not knowledge. The really important problems are not the problems of the laboratory, but those of the heart. And it doesn't make any difference if you live on your Earth or mine. We all share the same universe," he said. "And we all have some kind of heart" — he smiled — "even if it's in our toes or ears." I gulped, wondering if his heart might be in his toe or his ear. "Whether your RV travels on the roads of Earth or on the roads between galaxies, the Prime Rule of the Universe is the same: Don't pick a fight with your traveling companions."

"It sounds like a pretty good rule," I said.

"And as for movies about peaceful space visitors, you might try *Chasm In The Ocean* or *Near Misses Of The Third Kind*." I reminded myself to see them again when they came on television next time. But mostly I was thinking about the Prime Rule, and Kathleen and Eddie, and my family. As if reading my mind he said, "I would like to meet your family. Mine is so far away."

"Sure," I said. "You could come to my house for dinner tomorrow. My parents won't mind. They like to meet my friends. Oh," I added, "maybe just don't tell them where you're from. I don't think they know about the Prime Rule yet."

⇌ Eight ⇋

When we came in the front door the next day, I could hear arguing going on in the kitchen. Mom and Penny. Something about red beets. Then Dad's angry voice chimed in. He started arguing about how much arguing goes on around here.

Penny came in from the kitchen with a bowl of red beets and slammed them on the dining room table. "Who's this?" she asked. "One of your little friends?" Without even waiting for an answer she stomped back into the kitchen.

Dad came out next. He turned on the news. "Who's your friend, Casey?"

A name. A name. I hadn't thought about that. But no matter, Dad was listening to the news. He seemed to have forgotten about his question.

"Who are they?" the friend with no name asked. "Your mother and father?"

"My sister and father. Penny just likes to *look* old." In the kitchen Mom was blending something. "Mom, can my friend stay for dinner?"

"Sure," she yelled over the noise. "Where do you live?" she asked. "I haven't seen you in the neighborhood, have I?"

"He's just visiting," I yelled back. "An RV over by the cemetery."

"Harvey? Glad to have you, Harvey," she yelled. "Sorry about the noise."

"That's all right," I muttered. "Somebody's always yelling about something around here." But I decided one thing right then and there: Harvey was my friend's name.

We all sat down in the dining room. Dad left the news on. The Granger bickering continued. No one makes allowances for company in *this* house.

Penny: "I don't have any clean clothes to wear tonight."

Mom: "Is that my fault? You know where the washer is, same as I do."

News: "Rioting continues in the war-torn capital of . . ."

Penny: "I hate this pasta. It's . . ."

Dad: "When you start helping out a little more around here, *then* you can complain. Where's the butter? Why isn't there any butter on the table?"

News: ". . . two were shot and killed during a robbery last night . . ."

Mom: "Why doesn't anyone in this family clean up in the bathroom after themselves? I'm always the one who has to pick up wet towels . . ."

News: "The latest peace agreement has failed and fighting has resumed . . ."

Dad: "I expect you home at a reasonable time tonight, Penny."

News: "Astronomers say its rate of expansion will tell us how old and how big the universe is. And the amount of dark matter in it will determine whether the universe will expand forever, or whether it will eventually collapse back on itself . . ."

Mom: "Casey, your room was in a shambles this morning. I could hardly find Bumps in there."

They were turning on me now. "Did you hear that?" I asked no one in particular. "The expansion of the universe. You just don't think about that every day. The universe is probably expanding right now, this minute, even while we eat these red beets. Hard to imagine, isn't it?"

"It's hard to imagine anything when you're eating red beets," Penny said.

"There's millions of stars," Mom said. "It's scary. I don't even want to think about the universe. It's too big." She shuddered like she was cold.

"Sextillions of stars," Harvey corrected.

"Uh, Harvey, we don't usually talk about that at the table," I explained to him in a whisper.

"You don't talk about stars at the table?" Harvey said.

"Stars?" I said.

"Precisely. In the universe," he said. "You could think of it as thousands of quintillions," he said, "or millions of quadrillions, or even billions of trillions. They all mean the same thing." He turned his hands palms up in an apologetic gesture. "I can't help it," he said with an impish smile. "There are often hundreds of billions of stars in just one galaxy. And there are hundreds of billions of galaxies," he said. "Do the math."

"I can't *imagine* it," I said clutching my head with both hands and opening my mouth as if to scream, in order to divert attention from The Boy Who Knew Too Much.

"Casey, we don't open our mouths at the table!" my father proclaimed.

"You don't?" Harvey said, completely mystified.

"Sorry, Dad," I said.

"You can't imagine something?" Penny said. "I can't imagine *that*!"

Everyone was looking at me. I was still clutching my head and, though I had closed my mouth, I started groaning now. "How can this be, how can this be?" I moaned. "And expanding, too!"

"Enough, Cassandra Ann," Mom said.

"Wait a minute!" Penny said. "We studied that in school one time. Red-shift and all that." She played with her pasta. "But I don't believe it. I mean, how can galaxies just keep getting bigger?"

Of course, Harvey had to answer. "To be more precise," he said to Penny, "galaxies aren't expanding." He speared a beet with his fork. "The universe *itself* is expanding," — Harvey arched one hand high over his head, exerting an expansive pull on the beet galaxy, which he raised slowly from his plate — "creating space as it goes, and *pulling* the galaxies along." He was very excited.

"So that's the beet theory of the week, huh?" Dad said.

"Oh, no. It's quite well proven," Harvey said, sticking the former galaxy into his mouth.

All eyes were glued on Harvey. Suspicious eyes. "His parents are both astronomers," I said quickly.

"And cosmologists," Harvey corrected. "Me, too. We study the nature of the universe."

"You study the nature of the universe with your parents?" Penny asked.

"My whole family does, even though most of them aren't scientists at all. What could be more interesting?"

"What's this stuff they were talking about on television?" Dad asked, and actually clicked the box off. "This dark stuff. What is it? Invisible?" He looked at Harvey.

"In a sense. It's invisible to your telescopes," Harvey said.

"We don't have any telescopes," Dad said.

"I didn't mean *your* telescopes," Harvey corrected. "I meant your scientists' telescopes."

"We don't have any scientists, either," Penny said. "Do we, Dad? Other than the mad scientist, I mean," she said, pointing at me. She and Dad laughed.

"Your *planet's* telescopes," Harvey said.

"*Our* planet, Harvey?" Mom laughed. "And what planet are *you* from?" She laughed. Everybody laughed. I pushed red beets around my plate and contemplated the fact that it takes someone from another galaxy to make my family laugh.

"From one far, far, away," Harvey said. More laughter. "To get back to your excellent question, Mr. Granger. Dark matter is too far away and too dim to see with your," — Harvey studied the faces studying him — "that is, *our*, present technology. Galaxies and stars, which are easy to see, make up less than 10% of all the matter in the universe. The rest of the universe is made up of dark matter. And there may be enough of it not only to *stop* the expansion of the universe, but to reverse it."

Penny's eyes were suddenly as big as flying saucers. "You mean the universe will start getting smaller some day?" she said in a panicky voice. "Smaller and smaller?"

"Possibly," Harvey agreed. "But someday many billions of years from now. Pass the red beets, please."

I was wondering why every number in this discussion was an -illion of some sort when the doorbell rang. I ignored it. For one of the few times in my life I was interested in seeing what was going to happen next at our dinner table. The bell rang again.

"See who's at the door please, Casey," Mom said. I raced to the door and flung it open: It was Eddie. What did *he* want?

"What do you want, Eddie? We're eating. Shouldn't you be eating too? Go home and eat at your house." I started to close the door.

"I wanted to say that I'm sorry." Sorry? Did I honestly hear Eddie Maskit say he was sorry? I opened the door a little.

"Did you say you were sorry, Eddie?"

"I'm sorry about that call last night. In fact, I'm sorry about the last few days. I want to be friends again."

"Okay, Eddie, we're friends again," I said, and started to close the door again. I had heard Harvey say something about a "Big Crunch." I wanted to know what *that* was.

"Who's that?" Eddie asked, straining to see into the dining room. "Who's that kid?"

"Nobody," I said.

"Where's he from? I never saw him before."

"He's visiting."

"Who? Who's visiting?"

"*He's* visiting, Eddie. Now be a friend. Go home."

"What's his name?"

"Harvey."

"Harvey what?"

"Harvey . . . uh . . . uh . . ." I stammered. Oh no. Now I was sounding like Eddie!

"Harvey Uhuh?"

"No, Eddie, not Harvey Uhuh. I've got to go. I've got company."

"Let me in. I want to tell you something."

"You wouldn't want to come in, Eddie. We're having beets." I gave him a push and closed the door.

"I love beets," Eddie said through the wood.

* * *

Later, when Harvey was leaving, we found Camomile waiting outside on the sidewalk. "Meow," she said.

"Good evening," Harvey answered.

"Meow, meow, meow," she said.

"Thank you. I will," Harvey said. Cam weaved in and out of Harvey' legs and then mine. Her bundle of black fur vanished into the shadows. "Cam invited me to come to her home tomorrow evening and visit with Terence and Sophie O'Toole," Harvey explained. "Friends of yours, I understand."

"They sure are. I'll meet you after school and take you over there."

"That's just what Cam suggested. I'm going to Antarctica during the day."

"Remember what I asked about Friday? About after school? Remember? Can I go with you somewhere on Friday?" He seemed to be thinking that over. "I haven't been hardly anywhere yet," I pleaded. "Not Antarctica, or hardly even Illinois. And I'd stay out of your way and be real quiet and —"

"I'm sure I would enjoy your company. Depends on where I'm going. I'll let you know."

I was so excited about taking a trip in a spaceship that I didn't pay good enough attention to what Harvey said next. Something about infrared, and he pointed toward the street. "I thought you were the only one who could do that," he said.

⇌ Nine ⇋

The next day school was almost over by the time Eddie even showed up. He was grinning in that evil way he has. I caught up to him in the hall.

"Decided to show up today? Kind of late, don't you think?" I asked. I sniffed and sniffed again. "What's that smell on you, Eddie?"

"Perceptive, Casey. I didn't know you had it in you. We burned leaves at my house this morning, if it's any of your concern."

"Still mad I didn't let you in last night and introduce you to my new friend?"

"You mean that weird kid who lives in that haunted house?"

"Eddie Maskit, what do you know about it?"

"Can I go with you on Friday?"

"No." I ducked into the bathroom. I was furious. Eddie must have been spying on Harvey and me last night while we talked outside. Then he must have followed Harvey back to the haunted house. I had to keep him out of my way until my Halloween surprise.

But Eddie wouldn't stay out of my way. He rode his bicycle around and around me as I walked home.

"You're going to get dizzy, Eddie, and end up loopier than you already are."

"Just let me go with you on Friday. I'll never bother you again if you let me."

Now there was a tempting offer. But I didn't believe it. I didn't think Eddie was capable of not bothering me. He'd been bothering me since kindergarten. I hurried into my house, hoping he'd leave. I had to meet Harvey at the haunted house and take him to The Lucky Leprechaun Shoe Shop. I didn't need Eddie for company. But ten minutes later he was still there, wearing out the street in front of my house. I called Kathleen.

"Your friend Eddie is hanging around my house. He won't leave. Come and get him," I told her.

"I'm not responsible for Eddie," she said. "Call his mother." She hung up. That was a good idea. Not *really* calling his mother but . . .

"Hey, Eddie," I called out the door, "I talked to your mother on the phone. She said you'd better stop hanging around here and go home right away."

"Sure, Casey."

"She sounded like she meant it."

"I'll bet," Eddie snickered.

"She called you Edward Algernon."

Eddie screeched to a stop, turned his bike around and zoomed away. I'd been saving this little trick for years. Eddie has always kept his middle name a secret. All that the world is supposed to know is that his middle initial is an A. Sometimes he tells people he doesn't *have* a middle name, just an initial. He probably got that idea from Mr. Harold T. Bumps. But I heard his mother call him Edward Algernon on the first day of kindergarten. Right after he pulled my hair for the very first time. I didn't forget it.

* * *

"Harvey, this is my favorite uncle, Uncle Terence," I said introducing them in the living room above the shoe shop. "Uncle Terence, this is my favorite alien, Harvey."

Sophie came in from the hallway at that moment. "Oh, my dear Casey, don't call him that. How can any of us be alien? We all live in the same universe." She offered her hand to Harvey. "Glad to meet you, Harvey. My name is Sophie."

Even though he looks like a kid, Sophie didn't treat Harvey like he was a child. She treated him like an equal. She treats everybody — including animals, and plants, and things — like an equal. She seemed to know about Harvey's Prime Rule already, and she'd only just met him!

"Your kindness makes this visitor from another galaxy so at home."

"Where *is* your home galaxy?" Uncle Terence asked. "Can we see it?"

"You call it M31, or Andromeda. It's a nearby galaxy in the Local Group, a sister to your Milky Way. And, as I've explained to Casey, you can see it if the conditions are right. Of course, observatories on Earth have taken many photographs of it with their huge telescopes. Like Mount Palomar, near San Diego. But even so, those images show Andromeda the way it looked two and a half million years ago."

"How could that be?" I almost shouted. "There weren't any cameras around that long ago." This was very weird. Sometimes I love weird.

"I don't think there were any *people* around that long ago, Casey," Uncle Terence said.

Sophie and I went to the window. A tiny sliver of moon hung in the darkening sky. "Isn't the moon looking gorgeous tonight," Sophie murmured.

"Yes, your moon is always wonderful," Harvey said. "Always the same, yet always changing. But you're not seeing it as it looks right now. You're seeing the moon as it looked a little over a second ago. That's because light takes time to get here. Tomorrow when you see the sun, you will see it as it was eight minutes before. The sun is much farther away than the moon.

"And when you look at the stars, think of this: It takes light from the stars that make up the Big Dipper about seventy-five *years* to get here. And the North Star, Polaris, you see not as it is now, but as it was about five hundred years before Columbus got lost on his way to India. Andromeda, at two and a half million light-years distance, looks like it did two and a half million years ago."

"It's like a time machine," Uncle Terence said.

"Precisely," Harvey said. "Every time you gaze at the sky, you are looking back in time."

* * *

"Uncle Terence?" I asked as he drove me home.

"Yes, Casey?"

"Would you chaperon my party Halloween night? It's going to be at Harvey's house, and only Kathleen and Eddie are coming. Our parents won't let us go to a party at a stranger's house unless someone they know is there."

"Just what do you have planned for that night?"

"I can't tell yet. Will you, though? You and Sophie?"

"Sophie and I will discuss it. Have you by any chance let Harvey in on the plan yet?"

"I will real soon."

"Well, Casey, that would be a proper first step. Then, I imagine, if he wants to have a party, we will come." Uncle Terence pulled into the driveway. I jumped out of the car before he could change his mind about the party. I was a step closer to giving my two ex-old friends the scare of their lives.

Before I went in I took another look into the night sky. Polaris twinkled with a light that was only halfway to earth when Christopher Columbus set sail. The universe was bigger and more mysterious than I had ever known.

⇌ Ten ⇋

The next day Eddie was acting normal. Too normal. It wasn't Eddie-like. He wasn't asking to go with Harvey and me tomorrow. He wasn't bothering me at all. Very un-Eddie-like.

Even after school Eddie was nowhere in sight, so I went directly over to Harvey's house. Leaves swirled around, and the shadows of clouds and trees played like spooks on the rough exterior of the building. Yes, I congratulated myself, the idea of having the Halloween party here was a stroke of genius.

Harvey was in the tower control room, checking the "speedometer on his pair of glasses." Or at least that's what it sounded like he said. And he had already finished synchronizing for the day. "Where would you like to go tomorrow?" he asked me.

"I was thinking about that mountain. The one where we could see your galaxy better."

"Mount Palomar. Yes, it's in the mountains north of San Diego. The telescope there is one of the biggest in the world."

"Could we go there?" I asked.

"We certainly could," said Harvey. "But there are always people working there, and I think the authorities would be suspicious of two 'kids' on their own."

"We could go invisible," I said. "I can bring you some magic soap. No one will know we're there and we could go wherever we want."

"Well, I've never been invisible. I shouldn't want to let that opportunity pass me by," Harvey said. "It's settled then. We'll go to Mount Palomar, and I'll show you Andromeda."

"I can hardly wait," I said. "Thanks, Harvey."

"Well, it's only one day away, Casey. I'm sure you can wait that long," he laughed. "But it's good that we're going so soon. I've just finished my measurements. The wormhole stability has decreased and I will have to return home sooner than I thought."

"How soon?" I said.

"According to the densometer reading on my paragalaxis here, the wormhole will be in position for my trip home only until Saturday night, October 31. Until precisely 11:59 and 59 seconds. If I miss it I might never get home again."

⇌ Eleven ⇋

Finally, school ended on Friday.

I gave Harvey a sliver of magic soap and told him how to use it, and hurried home to use some myself. It seemed to me that the bar of soap was getting smaller awfully fast, but I was too excited about my trip with Harvey to worry about it.

When I got to the RV there was no sign of Harvey. My invisible feet flew up the steps into the control room. "Harvey! Harvey!" I called and threw myself into one of the chairs. Right on top of a body, an invisible body. "Yeow!" the body yelled, and stood up. I dropped off onto the floor, which made me yell, too. "Harvey?" I whispered.

"Oh my liver, Casey. You almost killed me."

It wasn't Harvey. It was Eddie. He was here in the shuttle and he was invisible. And he was stealing my line! What worse could possibly happen?

"Eddie? What are you doing here, Eddie? What? Did you watch *Stowaway To One Of Those Many, Many Moons Of Jupiter* last night and decide to stowaway, too? Do you know how *stupid* that movie is, Eddie?"

"Wrong again, Casey," he said, which made me wonder when I'd ever been wrong before. "The movie was called *Kid Brother From Another Planet*. It's about this outer spaceman who's hanging around on Earth. Just like Harvey.

Which reminds me, Casey, how could you keep all this a secret from your best friend?" Eddie nearly yelled.

"I guess I didn't, or you wouldn't be here now. And, besides, you're not my best friend, Eddie. Kathleen's my best friend."

"I know," he said, "that you *pretend* Kathleen's your best friend. Anyway, you haven't told Kathleen, either. How could you even think or try or *hope* to keep such an incredible secret from us? A spaceship from another galaxy. What kind of best friend are you, anyway?!"

"You guys were keeping secrets too," I reminded him. "And stealing. How else would you be here invisible? I *thought* my soap was getting too small."

"I almost told you that night you were having beets. Remember? I wanted to come in and tell you something, but you slammed the door in my face? Remember?"

"Yes, yes," I said impatiently.

"I was going to tell you that we got some of your soap but you wouldn't listen."

"So telling me you stole my soap would make everything okay?"

"Well it would be better than finding out like this, wouldn't it? Anyway, you wouldn't listen. So I spied on you and Harvey when you were talking about going on a trip today. And I found out that Harvey isn't just a new kid in town. He *is* The Kid Brother From Another Planet."

"Yeah, I remember now. Harvey said he saw someone with just infrared showing. I should have paid more attention. And because of that I have to be bothered by you again, and on the most exciting day of my life!"

"Your detective skills must be slipping, Casey," Eddie said. "The next day you even noticed I smelled funny, remember?"

"Yes, yes," I said irritably. "I remember."

"Being invisible isn't that easy."

"Tell me about it," I said.

"I had to stay home from school until I became visible again, and even then that lingering odor could have given me away."

"Rub it in, Eddie," I said.

"Sorry," Eddie said. "Kathleen said we should be very careful how and when we used the soap."

"Kathleen said 'we'? As in *she* was going to use the soap? I don't think so, Eddie. Kathleen is completely scared of being invisible."

"Are you sure, Casey?" A voice that sounded suspiciously like Kathleen's came from across the room. "Okay, I am scared, but I guess not completely."

"Kathleen?" It couldn't be.

"You can't see me, can you?" she challenged.

"No, but I still can't believe it," I said.

"I took some of your soap. You'd been threatening to scare us to death at your Halloween party so we decided to get invisible and scare you instead." She giggled. "I can't believe I did that. Or this. Look at me."

"I'm trying."

"You can't see me, can you?" she asked again, but this time she sounded worried.

"The night of the storm." I snapped my invisible fingers. "You were in the hall. You said you were looking for coffee. How dumb can I be?"

"Well there was that time —"

"Never mind," I interrupted. "You were upstairs in my room. Stealing. I thought I heard someone on the stairs. And Eddie was trying to keep me occupied on the phone."

"That's right," Eddie said as if he deserved a prize.

"Don't get a big head, Eddie. You didn't fool me. What really kept me from figuring it out was the fact that I never in a million years would have suspected that Kathleen would go sneaking around in someone's house. But I guess I was wrong about that."

Harvey came in. He was still visible. "*There* you are, Harvey," I said. "But you're still visible. What's wrong? Aren't we going?"

"Hasn't worked yet," he said. "My metabolism's mixed up. I'm really quite old." No sooner had he spoken, than poof! He vanished. Faster than I'd ever seen it happen. "We'd better take off," he said. "I'm not sure how long this will last on me. I see we have two new passengers."

"This — wherever they are — is Eddie and Kathleen," I said.

"Welcome aboard," Harvey said. "Make yourselves comfortable." Two more chairs popped out of the floor. "Shall we embark?" Harvey asked.

"Embark?" I said.

"Blast off?" he said.

"Sure, let's go!" said Eddie.

"Yes, let's blast off," Kathleen said.

"Casey? Are you ready?" Harvey asked.

I didn't really want Eddie and Kathleen along, especially after they tricked me, but I had to hand it to them — they had tricked me good. "I'd better be," I said. "This was my idea. Remember, *I* created all you monsters. *I* found the magic soap. You wouldn't be invisible if it weren't for me."

"Remind us to thank you later, Dr. Frankenstein," Kathleen said.

"Don't forget the Prime Rule of the Universe," Harvey said. "Don't fight with your traveling companions."

"Yeah," I said. "No fighting, you guys."

"Well you started it," Eddie said.

"I did not. *You* did, when —"

"Uh, guys?" Kathleen interrupted.

"Thank you, Kathleen," Harvey said. "Okay. Let's try again. Everybody ready?"

"Yes."

"Ready."

"Yep."

A lever near the screen moved down. "Blast off!"

And we did. Green light flooded the room. We were above the trees, above St. Louis, above the clouds. All in a few seconds. Physically, I didn't feel anything. Emotionally, I'd left my stomach down on the ground.

Then we were out of the clouds, flying high over what looked like a quilt made of the Earth and heading for very bumpy patches just ahead. "There went Missouri and Kansas. Colorado Rocky Mountains straight ahead," Harvey said. We flew over hundreds of snowy, steepled mountains. Then we veered left. The mountains smoothed out, giving way first to softer hills and mighty canyons and then to dry flat desert. "Utah, Arizona," Harvey sang out. A few small mountains passed almost before Harvey could say, "California here we come!"

Then, in a flash, all was blue. All around, above and below. "The Pacific Ocean," Harvey said. "One of the great wonders of your world."

We dropped to a few yards above the waves. Blue rolled on and on beneath us. "Wow," Kathleen said.

Harvey turned the shuttle around and we headed for land. Seals played on rocks near shore. "Cool," Eddie said.

"Come over here, Casey," Harvey said, "I want you to take us the rest of the way to Mount Palomar."

"Oh my liver," I said.

⇌ Twelve ⇋

I sat at the controls. I must be dreaming, I thought. We skimmed over hills toward the ridge of a mountain topped by a huge, white, domed building.

"Palomar Observatory," Harvey said. "Take it down, Casey." He guided my hands on the controls and we slipped down over the side of the ridge to a small clearing. "Now," he said, "in order to get back to the RV, all we have to do is press the reset button and the ship will take us back automatically." A hand — Harvey's hand, suddenly visible — pointed at a glowing green circle on the control panel. The hand disappeared. His other hand came into view for a moment. Then it, too, faded back into invisibility.

"Can I push it?" Eddie said.

"Can I?" asked Kathleen.

"Well, nobody better push it. We just got here," I said.

We got out of the shuttle. The big white observatory overshadowed everything around. "Looks like a giant's vanilla ice cream cone," Eddie said.

Harvey said, "Looks like the most beautiful observatory on this planet."

Looks like a snow-covered mountain, one I want to climb, I thought as I headed toward it. Eddie must have been heading for it, too, because we crashed into each other.

"Wait, Casey and Eddie," Harvey said. I couldn't see anyone, but Harvey could see all of us, I guess, because of our infrared. "Hold hands, everyone. That way we'll all know where everyone is."

"And maybe Casey will stop stepping on my foot," Eddie said pulling his toes out from under my sneaker. I found Eddie's hand and Harvey found mine.

"Kathleen, where are you?" I called quietly. I hadn't heard from her since we got off the ship.

Kathleen's voice came from nearby. "I can't believe I'm here . . . on this ship . . . I hope nobody finds it while we're gone . . . maybe I should stay and watch it . . . no, I want to see the telescope . . . I can't believe I'm here," she said again. "And invisible . . . and with a . . . a . . ."

"Don't say it, Kathleen," I said. "Harvey is a friend, not an alien."

"You're right, Casey. Sorry, Harvey."

"That's all right," said Harvey. "Anyway, I don't feel like a stranger, not with so many new friends."

"Thanks," Kathleen said.

"Come on over here and hold on to Eddie. We're going to the museum first. I want to show all of you a photo of the galaxy I come from." He pointed to a building near the observatory.

"Remember," I said as we got closer to the door, "people can't see us but they can hear us, so be *extra* quiet."

"Quiet as a moose in a church," Harvey said.

"A mouse," I whispered.

"Precisely," Harvey whispered back.

We dragged along, holding hands, and except for Harvey, each of us blind to the others. We bounced off each other like billiard balls. Despite my order, our trek to the museum was peppered with whispered complaints and commands.

"That was my toe somebody stepped on."

"Watch out for my shoulder, please." Of course, nobody could watch out for anybody's shoulders.

"Keep your elbows in your own ribs, Casey."

"Ow, Eddie. Ow, Eddie. Ow, Eddie! *Quit it*, Eddie!"

It was late in the afternoon, and luckily there was nobody nearby. Almost nobody anywhere, really. Finally, we got to the museum and went in. It was a large, dimly lit room, and cool enough to make me shiver. There were photos of galaxies on the walls. The largest photo was on the front wall. "Andromeda Galaxy" said the sign under the picture. It was a beautiful swirl of light in the black of outer space.

"That's where I live," Harvey said. "Andromeda is a spiral galaxy, which means its stars are arranged in the shape of a spiral. It's much like your Milky Way, although a bit larger and more tightly wound."

"Wound?" I asked. "You mean like a spring in a toy?"

"More like an ice skater in a spin," Harvey said. "One with his arms out more, that's the Milky Way. The other, with arms closer in, that's Andromeda."

Two men came in, workers I guessed from their uniforms. "Everybody out?" said one. His voice echoed like thunder off the walls.

"I don't see anybody," boomed the other. "Let's lock 'er up."

"Yeah. Hey, Jim," said the first man, "don't forget about cleaning up that oil in the 'scope room. Steve said the bearing's leaking again."

"Got it," Jim replied.

We rushed to the door, so as not to get locked in. This time we were more like moose than mice. One of the men said, "You think it could be Hale's Elf?" The other laughed, and they locked the door behind them. We kept still until they drove away in their white truck.

"What's hailzelf?" I asked Harvey.

"Hale's Elf." Harvey said the words slowly. "They were talking about George Hale, the man who built the telescope in the main observatory. A legend says that he was told to build it by a very annoying elf that wouldn't leave him alone."

"Kind of like you, Eddie," I said. "Always there when you don't want him. Always snooping around. Very annoying. Always —"

"Hold on," Kathleen interrupted. "You're the one who was snooping around my basement."

"And you're the one," I said, "who snooped in my room. And Eddie's the one who snooped on Harvey."

"Stop!" Harvey whispered in no uncertain terms. "Need I remind you of the Rule?" he asked. We all assured him that he didn't. "Good. Join hands, then." We did. I guess we'd let go during the argument. "Now. Look at that," Harvey urged. We had come around some trees and suddenly the main observatory was before us. It looked much bigger close up. "Prepare yourselves," Harvey said. "Inside that building you are going to see one of the finest examples of one of the greatest inventions of your species. A telescope. It can take us on a journey. And not only a journey to far, far from here," he said, "but a journey to long, long *ago*. A journey not only into space but into time.

"What do you mean?" Kathleen said.

"It's about light, Kathleen," I said. "See, light is what makes us see, and light takes time to get here. So the light shows you what something looked like when . . . let's see, *how* does that work again, Harvey?"

"It shows you what something looked like when the light left the object. From close things light gets to you fast. But from far away things — like planets, and stars, and galaxies — even light, fast as it is, can take quite a while to get to you. Astronomers call it Lookback Time, because they are always seeing things the way they *used* to look. If we are very lucky tonight, maybe we can see what the astronomers here see when they look out into space with this telescope. Galaxies millions, even billions of light-years away. Which means seeing them millions or billions of years ago."

We had been following a sidewalk that had led us to the door of the observatory, which rose before us now like a huge, round, gleaming-white temple.

We climbed steps into the building. Then we climbed more steps and more steps and more steps inside. Nobody was coming down, thank goodness, or they would have collided with us. The stairs finally ended at a small room. A man and a little girl were in there. We tiptoed in. One wall was made of glass. It looked into another room, round and much bigger than the first. The telescope was in there, and much larger than I had imagined. It reached high into the dome, far, far over our heads.

"Oh my liver," I said.

"Wow," Eddie said.

The man and the girl looked at each other. "Did you say that?" each one asked the other. Then they shrugged and looked back at the telescope.

"The mirror on this telescope is 200 inches across. That's more than sixteen *feet*, Jen!" the man read excitedly from a small pamphlet. "The dome is seven stories high."

"Wow," Eddie said again.

Two sets of astonished eyes turned in our direction again. At that moment Jim, the man from the museum, appeared at the head of the stairs. "Something wrong?" he asked the man and girl. They looked like they had seen a ghost.

"We keep thinking we hear somebody over there," the man said. I could tell he was embarrassed.

"He says 'wow'," the girl added, "huh, Dad."

"I'm sure it's nothing," her father said to the museum worker, gesturing to the empty room. "Probably just the wind, or an echo or something."

". . . an echo, an echo, an echo . . ." Eddie said. I could have killed him.

"Hmmph," Jim said. "Must be that ol' Hale's Elf again. Anyway, time to close the viewing gallery. Sorry, but you folks'll have to leave. You can come back tomorrow if you want." The three of them took off down the long flight of stairs, their voices trailing back up to us.

"What did you think of the telescope, Jen?"

"Wow," came the little girl's reply. "Hey, Dad, is there really an elf up there?"

I could hear both of the men chuckle. "Well, now, nobody rightly knows." It was Jim's voice. "Hale was the fella who had the idea about buildin' this telescope. That's why they call it the Hale Telescope. Now the story goes that there was this little elf who kept whisp'rin' in his ear, and it was —"

"Was he a friend of Santa Claus?"

"Who?" Jim asked.

"The man with the elf."

I heard the outside door close behind them and they were gone. I wondered what the answer to her question was.

On the other side of the glass, where the telescope was, a man and a woman came up a staircase. They went into a room. I could see computer monitors inside. "Those two are most likely astronomers," Harvey said. "I'd like to get into that room."

"Shh," I said. Footsteps were coming up the long flight of steps from the front door again.

"I thought the place was closing. Who could that be?" wondered Kathleen in a whisper.

"Shh," I repeated.

It was Jim, the museum man, again. He must have locked the door behind the visitors and come back up. He picked up a couple of pieces of trash and unlocked a door that led right into the telescope room. On an impulse I squeezed behind him. Everybody else must have had the same idea. We couldn't have done it better if we'd planned it for a month. A moment later the door clanged shut. We were in.

The room was round, silver-walled, and shiny. The huge telescope pointed straight up, jutting nearly to the top of the dome, which was way, way higher than the ceiling in any room I'd ever been in before. It made me dizzy to look up at it.

We had let go of hands as we squeezed through the door with Jim, who was heading for the telescope. Kathleen and Eddie and I found each other quickly enough, but where was Harvey? Just then I got an answer. Harvey was across the room, a few feet away from the door the astronomers had entered, the room Harvey had said he wanted to see.

Only now he was visible.

⇌ Thirteen ⇋

"What's that boy doing in here?" Jim said. "It's past closing time." He was standing near the telescope and seemed almost to be talking to himself. But then two heads poked out of the door of the room Harvey was headed toward. "Is he with one of you?" Jim said.

"No," said the male astronomer.

"Where did he come from?" said the woman, as they all gathered around Harvey. "Where is your mom or dad?"

"Far away," Harvey answered.

"Who did you come with then?" she asked.

"Some new friends of mine."

"And where are they?"

"Did they leave without you?" the other astronomer asked.

"They're over there somewhere." Harvey pointed in our direction.

"I don't see anything," Jim said.

"They're invisible to you," Harvey said. "I can only see their —"

I jumped up and down and kicked at the door, making a terrible racket so that no one would hear about invisible kids and infrared.

"What was *that*?" Jim said.

"Jim, will you see if there are any visitors left?" said the lady.

Jim left by the door into the viewing gallery, missing me by less than a foot. I watched him through the glass as he looked around the empty room and then went down the stairs. A door slammed.

"How did you get in here?" It was the male astronomer again, talking to Harvey.

"I followed that man in through that door."

"That's impossible."

"Well, that might be putting it a little strong, Steve," said the female astronomer. "I mean, we spend our lives looking at stars and galaxies that may not even exist anymore! Who can say what's impossible?"

Pounding on the gallery stairs again, and a moment later Jim burst in through the door. He called to the astronomers from across the wide, circular room. "I couldn't find anybody. And there aren't any cars left in the parking lot. You want me to call the cops?"

"What do you think, Carol?" Steve said.

No! No! I wanted to yell.

"I guess we'd better report it," Carol said. "Somebody's probably hysterical already, looking for him."

"It will take them at least an hour to get up here," Jim said.

"He can stay with us in the meantime," Carol said. "What's your name?" she asked Harvey.

"My friends here call me Harvey."

"What's your last name?"

"On your planet Harvey is my first, last and only name. I'd like to go in there, please." Harvey pointed to the astronomers' work room.

"Your name is Harvey Harvey?" Steve said.

"On *our* planet?" Carol said.

"I'm calling the police," Jim said. Then he was gone, disappearing down the stairway the astronomers had first come in by.

This was trouble. We had to act fast and get Harvey out of here before the police came and took him away to who knows where to find his parents. That could take a very long time! Harvey would miss his wormhole back to Andromeda. Harvey didn't look upset, though. In fact, he looked pretty excited as he followed the astronomers into their little room.

"Casey?" I jumped. It was Eddie, right next to me.

"What?"

"We've got to do something," he said.

"Yeah," said Kathleen. I could hear her foot tapping nearby. "But what? The police will be here in an hour. They'll take Harvey away."

"I know, I know," I said. "Stop tapping your foot, Kathleen. It's echoing all over the place." Kathleen stopped. "I'm going to try to get in there and talk to him," I said. "You guys stay here where we can find you again. And be quiet."

From the doorway of the astronomers' room I saw Harvey swivelling happily in a chair in front of some computer screens, watching the astronomers. They seemed distracted enough, talking to each other and keyboarding. I cleared my throat to get his attention. No reaction. I tiptoed in and tapped his arm. "What are we going to do?" I whispered.

"About what?" Harvey whispered back.

"About the police, Harvey, the police. They'll want to find your parents."

Harvey was silent a moment. "Perhaps we could find them ourselves," he said.

"What?"

"Casey, go get Terence and Sophie."

"Why?" I asked.

"Perhaps they could *be* my parents," he answered.

"Sophie and Uncle Terence are in St. Louis," I said.

"Take the shuttle," Harvey whispered.

"But . . ."

"Just push the reset button," Harvey said. "You can do it."

I scooted out and walked right into Kathleen and Eddie near the foot of the telescope. They had moved. "Ow, ow, ow," everyone said. Then, "Shh, shh, shh."

"Listen," I told them, "Harvey told me to take the shuttle and bring back Uncle Terence and Sophie."

"Good plan, the Uncle Terence and Sophie part," Kathleen said. "But you taking the shuttle? I don't think so."

"I've got to. It's all set to go back. Remember. I just need to push a button."

"I should go with you," Eddie said. "Kathleen can stay here to keep an eye on the situation."

"Yeah, but if they take Harvey someplace else, one of you needs to stay here and someone needs to go with him," I said. "So I have to go alone."

"Shouldn't we get a pilot or something?" Kathleen said.

"I don't think so, Kathleen. I don't think we have time to find a pilot with a license to fly a haunted house tower space shuttle."

"You're probably right," Kathleen said. "You'll have to go alone."

"Good luck," Eddie said.

Now that they agreed with me, I didn't want to go all by myself. I wanted my friends with me. But we had to work together. And Harvey needed them here. "Bye," I said quickly, and rushed out the door into the gallery. I stopped for a second and actually turned back and tried the doorknob. The door was locked. There was no going back. I was on my own.

⇌ Fourteen ⇋

I ran down the long flight of stairs as quickly and quietly as I could. The heavy entry door opened and let me out into the late afternoon. The sun was just slipping below the horizon.

The shuttle was just where we had left it, days ago it seemed. I climbed in, sat in Harvey's chair and stared at the controls. One of them was the return button. But which one? The green, I think it was. I took a deep breath, closed my eyes, and pushed it. When I opened my eyes a few seconds later I was in the sky and scudding over mountains into the darkness.

I landed just where we had started, on top of the old haunted house RV. I whispered a thank you to the shuttle and headed for the stairs. Then I remembered that I had to get to Uncle Terence's shop as fast as possible. But it would take a lot of time on foot. I remembered the control that Harvey had used to get me over to Uncle Terence's apartment the first night I had met Harvey. I returned to my seat and flicked the map switch.

Immediately, a map of Uncle Terence's neighborhood appeared on the wall. I pushed the orange button, then jabbed my finger where I thought the Lucky Leprechaun Shoe Shop would be. I wasn't in the shuttle anymore. But I wasn't in the shoe shop either, and I certainly wasn't in Uncle Terence's apartment. I was in a dark dirty basement.

Not Uncle Terence's basement, either. Where am I? I wondered. What have I done?

I followed a rickety staircase up to a heavy wooden door. A heavy *locked* wooden door. I put my ear to the door and listened. By the screeching sounds coming through the door I was pretty sure I knew where I was: the Play It Again Music Store, right next to Uncle Terence's shop. It sounded like someone was torturing a violin. Probably the same kid I'd seen in the store last summer. He hadn't improved one bit.

I pounded on the door. *Screech, screech* was all I got from the other side. I kicked at the door. *Screech, screech,* like fingernails on a chalkboard. I gritted my teeth. I couldn't stand this much longer. And I had to get help for Harvey.

"Let me out!" I yelled. "Let me out!"

The screeching stopped. "What's that?" I heard a small voice ask. It was the kid all right. "I don't know," he answered himself. "There's not supposed to be anyone here."

I wondered where Mr. Hoffman, the shop owner, was. "Let me out!" I hollered again. "I'm locked in the basement!"

I could hear the violin being set down, not too gently, then feet shuffling to the door. From my vantage point two steps down I could see very small shoes through the two inches of space under the door.

"Is somebody there?" the boy asked in a shaky voice.

"Yes. Let me out," I answered.

"Who put you in?" the boy asked.

"Nobody. Just let me out."

"Somebody did. How do I know you're not a monster?"

"I'm just stuck in here. I'm not a monster."

"Then what are you?"

"I'm a girl."

"What if you're not? What if you're the basement monster Mr. Hoffman told me about when he said not to go down the basement or even open the door? What if you're just using a girl's voice to fool me?"

"I'm *not* fooling," I said. "Where *is* Mr. Hoffman, anyway?"

"He broke a filling gritting his teeth during my lesson. Then he yelled a lot. He had to go to the dentist."

"Look, kid, I'm not a monster. And there are absolutely no monsters down here. Now let me *out*."

"How did you get in there then?"

The kid was starting to drive me crazy. "The truth is, I touched the wrong spot on the wall and my friend's spaceship brought me here by mistake."

"Oh. Okay." The latch slid and the door opened. The little violin torturer gaped at the empty space in front of him.

"Thanks," I said as I rushed by him and out the back door into the alley.

"An invisible spaceman!" I heard him yell. "Mr. Hoffman's going to be surprised!"

⇌ Fifteen ⇋

I let myself in the back door of the Lucky Leprechaun Shoe Shop. Uncle Terence and Sophie weren't there. Upstairs no one was at home either, except Camomile. She jumped into my invisible arms and threw me off balance. I landed on the couch with Cam on my lap. I think that was her intention.

"Cam, where's Uncle Terence? Where's Sophie?"

"Meow."

Time was running out fast. Jim had said an hour before the police would come. At least half of that time had passed. I had to figure out what to do and it looked like I was on my own. No Uncle Terence or Sophie to help this time. No Kathleen. No Eddie.

I petted Cam's long, silky fur and tried to think. She purred, and looked up at me as if to ask, What's the problem? "I've got to get Harvey out of the observatory before the police take him somewhere that will make him miss the wormhole tomorrow night," I told her. "The problem is he's turned visible, and they've seen him. I came back to get Sophie and Uncle Terence and . . . Wait a minute! I just have to get him invisible long enough to get him back to the shuttle. The soap! I've got to get the soap." Cam meowed in agreement and jumped off my lap. I think she knew I had to leave, and leave now.

Running to my house I worked out a plan. At home I found the little plastic spray bottle, the one we use to mist our plants. I put a sliver of magic soap and some hot water in it and shook it up. Magic water! I would "mist" Harvey back to invisibility. I only hoped it would last on him long enough to get him out of the observatory. On my way to the cemetery and the RV I stopped just long enough to splash some of the magic water on the outside of the bottle. In twenty minutes it would be invisible, too.

Back at the shuttle I had a new problem: How to get back to Mount Palomar. I figured the reset button I had pushed to get me here couldn't get me here *again*, so it would be safe to try. And, hopefully, it would take me back to Palomar. It did. I was back in the same clearing in a flash.

I felt awfully proud of myself as I headed up to the door of the observatory in the near dark. I had worked the shuttle all by myself and figured out a plan to get Harvey out of here. All that was left was to go inside now and save him. I pulled on the handle. The door was locked.

I'd forgotten it was past closing time. I ran around the building looking for another way in. And I got more scared when I saw a white car driving up. Was it the police? Was I too late?

Then I saw it. A door. A sign on it read "NO ADMITTANCE." The white vehicle pulled up. It was a pickup, not a police car. Jim got out and walked right toward the door. I followed him in.

I was in the bottom floor of the observatory. It was just like a big basement. It was huge and dark and round. Red steel girders, like the ones you see on old bridges, stretched between the floor and the ceiling. Holding up the telescope, I guessed. The place smelled like a workshop, and it was filled with barrels and boxes, and stacks of things I couldn't even name. One thing did catch my attention, though. It was a large drum. The label said "Flying Dragon," and beneath the picture of a dragon with wings the words "telescope oil" were written in felt marker.

Jim disappeared through a door. I didn't know where it went. I just knew that I had to get up to the level with the telescope, to where Harvey and Kathleen and Eddie were. We had climbed a lot of stairs to get there the first time. I found a staircase and climbed up and up until I saw the telescope. The astronomers' room was next to the stairs. At the doorway I bumped into Kathleen and Eddie. "It's me," I said. "What's happening?"

"Oh, Casey, thank goodness you're back. Where's Uncle Terence?" Kathleen said.

"And Sophie," Eddie said.

"I couldn't find them, but I've got some soap spray. I'm going to make Harvey invisible again so we can get him out of here."

"I don't think he wants to go. They've been talking in there like old friends," Eddie said.

"Well, I'm going in there and I'm going to spray some magic soap water on him, so be prepared. I don't know how long it will take to work. I'm hoping that being in a spray mist it'll work faster. Wait for us by that first door we came in. Okay? And be ready."

"Okay."

"Okay."

I went in. Steve and Carol and Harvey were sitting in front of a row of computer screens. They were all leaning back in their chairs, legs crossed with feet on the desks in front of them. They looked like three very relaxed astronauts, ready for take-off. Carol was talking.

"Now tell me again, Steve. You don't think there is *any* other life in *any* of the billions of galaxies in this universe?"

"Oh, I'm sure there is!" Harvey said enthusiastically.

"Unlikely," Steve said, "and even if there is life in a few of them, we'll never see it."

"Because those galaxies are billions of light-years away," Harvey said. "So if there is intelligent life somewhere, and if they could travel even at the speed of light, it would still take them billions of years to get here."

"Exactly," Steve said. "What grade are you in, anyway?"

"Unless, of course, the inhabitants of those galaxies found a faster way to travel," Harvey said. "You know, black holes, wormholes, any kind of holes. And of course there are closer galaxies," he said. "Andromeda, for example. Right here in our Local Group." I pointed my spray bottle and misted him. "What are you doing, Casey?" he said. "I'm all wet."

The two astronomers looked at each other and then back at Harvey.

"Now as I was saying," Harvey continued as though nothing had just happened, "let's suppose intelligent life *does* exist in Andromeda. And what if there *is* a way to bend time and space so that —"

"Wormholes are very theoretical," Steve said. "Very unlikely."

"But not impossible," Carol reminded him. "Hundreds of billions of galaxies . . ." She turned suddenly and said straight out to Harvey: "Just who in the universe *are* you, Harvey?"

"I'm trying to tell you," he said. And at that very moment, Harvey disappeared.

⇌ Sixteen ⇋

I grabbed hold of Harvey and pulled him to the door.

"Where'd he go?" Carol exclaimed.

"Who *is* that kid, anyway?" Steve demanded.

I hurried toward the viewing gallery door, Harvey in tow, but the way was blocked. Two policemen were coming up. Jim was with them. Backing away from the door just as it swung open toward us, we flattened against some cabinetry with a *thud.*

"What was that?" the first policeman said as he came through the doorway.

"I don't know," his partner answered. "The door must have banged against the wall, or these cabinets here." Suddenly his eye was caught by the huge telescope. "Whoa! Would you look at that thing!" he said.

"Be careful, Frank. Sarge said if we break the telescope, we bought it." He looked up at the machine looming above us all like a jumbo Tyrannosaurus and swallowed hard. "And I don't think we can afford it."

They headed toward the astronomers' work room. I waited until I thought they were out of earshot. "Let's go!" I whispered, hoping my friends could all hear me. "Now's our chance." I could hear Eddie and Kathleen nearby, but I'd let go of Harvey's hand and somehow lost track of him. I felt around and around for his hand, like someone trying to capture a butterfly. A black butterfly. In a dark room. "Harvey," I rasped. "Where are you?"

"Over here." Harvey's voice sounded far away. I scanned the broad empty space that lay between me and the work room. The two officers were almost across the area, just a few steps from the lighted doorway and the astronomers inside. And half way between me and them was Harvey, fully visible again, and heading exactly in the wrong direction.

"What was that?" said one of the policemen at the sound of Harvey's voice.

"It was me," Harvey said to the policemen's backs. Both men turned just as I began a shortest-distance-between-two-points-is-a-straight-line sprint towards Harvey. It took me directly under the telescope. At the last split second I saw it: Smack dab under the telescope was a little puddle of shiny, slippery oil. What with all the commotion, Jim hadn't cleaned it up.

"Yeooww!" I yelled involuntarily as my legs went out from under me. I had a feeling I knew now why they called it Flying Dragon. When I hit the ground again I dropped the spray bottle, went into a feet-first slide, skidded across the smooth floor, and took Harvey off his feet as though he were Eddie Maskit playing second base. Harvey fell forward, clutching at a policeman's belt as he went down. It was a chain reaction. A moment later both policemen, Jim, and Harvey lay in a wavy line across the floor like fallen dominoes. And I was the first domino — the invisible one.

"Excuse me," Harvey said again as he got up off the floor.

"Say, are you the kid they called us about?" the policeman named Frank asked. By this time I had found my spray bottle. I spritzed Harvey again, but good this time.

"Yes and no. You see, gentlemen officers of the law, it's not quite the way it looks."

"Just how do you mean, young fella?" asked gentleman officer #1, pulling himself to his feet.

"Well, you see, there is no genuine cause for alarm. I realize it appears to you that I am a lost Earth child, but I really am quite capable of taking care —"

"Hey! Where'd he go?" all three men yelled at once. Their words thundered through the building and echoed off the shiny, curved metal walls of the cavernous room.

Harvey had disappeared again. By luck I latched onto his arm and yanked him toward the nearest stairway. Harvey resisted.

"Wait," he complained. "Just a minute, Casey."

"Not now," I said, and kept pulling. "And keep your voice down."

"But, Casey," he whispered, "what are you doing? We didn't accomplish what we came for. Andromeda. I told you I would show you Andromeda."

"You did. In the museum, remember? Now let's get out of here before we get caught."

"But that was just a photo, Casey. No, I brought you here to *see* Andromeda."

It took a minute for that to sink in. "You mean *see*?"

"Precisely," he said.

"Like, through the telescope?"

"Yes. Through the looking glass, as it were."

"How can we do that?" I asked.

"Well, Sophie and Terence being here should satisfy the police. And I had hoped to persuade one of those nice young astronomers to help us get a look at Andromeda. That was before you burst in on us, and — by the way, where *are* Sophie and Terence?"

"I couldn't find them. That's why I sprayed you with the magic soap spray. So we could get you away."

"Oh. I see. *That's* what you were doing back there. And Sophie and Terence aren't here after all. Hmm. That does change things, doesn't it."

"I don't think you should be turning yourself in so much, for one thing," I said.

"I believe you are correct. Still, things might work out well. Everyone seems preoccupied now. We can just do it ourselves."

"Do what ourselves?"

"It won't be very difficult. First, of course, I'll have to program the computer to lock on M31 —"

"Andromeda?"

"Precisely. And then I'll instruct it to delay slewing the telescope for about five minutes. That should give us enough time."

"Time for what?" I asked.

"To get into prime focus."

I seemed to be losing the thread of the conversation. "What are we talking about?" I asked. "Why do we have to slay the telescope, and how can we get in focus when we're invisible to begin with, and what good is a dead telescope, anyway?"

"Ah, yes. Very good. To address your first and last questions, 'slewing' is an astronomy word. It just means 'moving' the telescope."

"Why not just say 'moving'?" I asked.

"An excellent question, and one I'm sure I cannot answer," he said. "At any rate, to see Andromeda we have to point it in the right spot. And 'prime focus' has nothing to do with us being seen or not seen. Prime focus is the part of a telescope where the image of the object one is viewing may be seen. In this case, prime focus is up there."

"Up where?" I asked.

He took my arm and pointed it toward the ceiling of the dome. "At the top of the telescope. There's a little room up there where you can look down the tube, and right out into the universe."

I was looking at the top of the telescope. It was taller than our big oak tree. But it wasn't like a tree at all. Trees are full of color and birds and handholds. You can climb trees. Trees are alive. But not the telescope. It was all glass and steel. Cold and smooth and grey and forbidding.

"I'm not sure this is such a good idea, Harvey. Everything's getting mixed up. Where are Kathleen and Eddie?"

"Oh, it's a *very* good idea," he assured me, ignoring my question. "I'll just ask them straight out: May we please have a look at Andromeda? If that doesn't work, well the police gentlemen seem to think I'm a little lost boy, and at least one or two people seem to think I just might be Mr. Hale's Elf. They're all very excited about our visit. If need be, I think we can use that to our advantage."

"I'm worried about the wormhole, Harvey."

"That's not until tomorrow night, Casey. We'll be done here in less than an hour. Invisibility should make it easy."

"Yeah. That's what *I* always say, too. What's your plan?"

"Okay. We'll go together, very quietly, into the astronomers' room. I'll start talking to one of them — which I think will get everyone's attention. If they honor my request, fine. If not, sooner or later one of them will approach us and that's when I want you to lead them on a chicken chase."

"A goose chase, you mean? A wild goose chase?"

"Precisely that."

"What if I get caught?"

"Oh, no, that wouldn't do. The idea is just to distract them a bit while I borrow the telescope and program it to our needs. That won't take long. Then, once you've gotten them confused enough and maybe a little out of breath, I want you to sneak up the staircase to that midlevel balcony." He pointed my arm again, this time at a wide sort of landing that completely encircled the main floor about a dozen feet over our heads. "I'll meet you there," he moved my arm again, "at the base of that ladder. See?"

"I see it," I said.

"We'll climb it together."

I reviewed the plan in my head. I studied the telescope, pointing perfectly upright there in the middle of the giant room, like a rocket. My eye traced the path of the flimsy ladder. It rose vertically at first along the wall of the dome. But as the dome curved, it did too. Anyone climbing it would be leaning forward more and more as they climbed up, with nothing but the slick steel of the ladder — and air — between them and the concrete floor below. About three-quarters of the way up there was a flat platform that reached over almost to the top of the telescope. It looked like a diving board with a railing.

Even I could see it was an impossible plan.

"Okay," I said.

⇌ Seventeen ⇋

Harvey and I crossed the empty room together. "So far, so good," I whispered.

"We haven't started yet," Harvey whispered back.

We entered the work room. Steve and Carol were there, along with the two police officers and Jim.

"Don't tell *me* I imagined him," Steve was saying to the first officer as we entered. "He was right here, talking to me. He knew a lot about astronomy and physics, too. He was smart."

"And then what happened?" the officer said.

"Then?" Steve hesitated. He looked around the room, as though he had mislaid Harvey somewhere and might spot him at any moment.

"Yes, then," the officer repeated.

"Then he disappeared," Steve fairly shouted. "And how can you say I imagined it, anyway? *You* heard him. *You* saw him yourself before he disappeared the second time."

"If I didn't know better, I'd say Hale's Elf has returned," Carol said.

"I don't know about you," Officer Frank spoke up, "but I don't make a habit of speaking to elves."

"Not a habit, perhaps, but surely on special occasions such as this!" Harvey said. Everyone in the room stopped talking. Everyone in the room stood absolutely still. "What's the matter, feline got everyone's tongue?" Harvey joked.

"Now, as I was trying to explain a bit earlier, the truth is I brought a friend with me. And really, all I wanted to do was show her the Andromeda Galaxy on your very beautiful instrument here. It wouldn't take but a few minutes."

"Where are you?" Officer Frank said.

"I'm right here, of course," Harvey said.

"Why can't we see you?" Steve asked.

"I'm afraid I don't know the answer to that. It's a bit of a surprising little gift from my friend."

"Where are you from?" It was Carol this time.

"I am from . . . Andromeda Galaxy," Harvey said. Gasps of shock came from every visible mouth in the room. I couldn't tell whether they were gasps of belief or of disbelief. Probably both. "I must return there soon," Harvey went on, "and I would like to show it to my friend before I go."

"What do you think, Steve?" Carol said.

"Andromeda?" said her co-worker.

"Oh, come on, Steve," Carol said. "Andromeda. That's *better* than an ordinary little old elf."

"What do *you* think, Fred?" Officer Frank asked his partner.

"I think somebody's pulling our leg," Officer Fred said, and lunged toward Harvey.

"Now!" Harvey shouted, and I heard him jump aside. "I'll meet you where we agreed!"

"Okay," I said, and darted toward the door. "Nyah-nyah, nyah-nyah, nyah nyah," I taunted. It had worked with the thugs who were trying to steal the magic soap formula last summer. And it worked just as well this time. A second later I was off and running. Jim and both cops were after me. I glanced over my shoulder and saw Steve in the light of the work room doorway. "Stop," he yelled to my pursuers. "You're going to break something! You'll get hurt!"

But they didn't stop. They ran, and ran, and ran. What they didn't know was that *I* had stopped. I had stopped by what looked like a big control panel of some sort, ten seconds after the chase began. It was kind of fun just to stand there and watch them circling the telescope, grabbing at thin air, trying not to run into each other.

"It's okay," Steve called to them again. "Let him go! He's not hurting anything."

I heard the sound of motors somewhere deep in the bowels of the building, and at that moment the dome began to open. A narrow slit of sky appeared in the rounded part of the dome, from the center of the ceiling down nearly to the landing. Quickly the slit grew wider, revealing a tall black rectangle of night sky. Dozens of points of starlight poked through. I tiptoed over to the staircase that led to the landing. I started up.

When I reached the landing at the top, I noticed something strange: The building was *moving*. Or at least part of it was. The floor I was standing on was like a wide balcony that ran around the entire observatory. It was divided into two parts by a small gap in the floor, a crack about half an inch wide. The inner part of the floor was still. But the outer part was moving, turning slowly along with the big dome toward a new part of the sky. Toward Andromeda, I was sure. I went over to the ladder and held on. There was still a lot of excitement below, but nobody seemed to have any idea what was going on, or what to do about it.

A moment later, Harvey was beside me. "Very good," he said. "We shouldn't have any trouble. I had a chance to explain a little better to Carol and Steve. They're all for us. Now, up you go." I stepped on the first rung. It made a soft ringing sound. The dome continued its slow spin. And the ladder with it.

"I'm scared," I said.

"It's fastened quite securely," Harvey said. "Perfectly safe. Carol and Steve tell me they've used it quite often. Do hold tight, however, and keep your mind on what you're doing."

"Okay," I said.

"Don't look down," he added. "Keep your eye on the ladder. One step at a time. I'm right behind you."

"Okay." I did look down once, but just for a second. Harvey was right.

"I'm going too slow," I worried to him halfway to the top. "I'm afraid the telescope will start moving before we get there."

"Don't worry," Harvey said. "I didn't have to program a delay. Remember, Carol and Steve are helping us on this. They won't move the telescope until I tell them we're ready."

"Okay," I said again, and kept on.

When we finally got to the top of the ladder we were able to swing off onto the diving board. I clenched the railing. It was flat and solid, though, and compared to the ladder it felt almost safe. We walked across it over to the top of the telescope. At Harvey's instruction, I stepped off the platform and onto — into, really — the telescope. I felt like I was loading myself into the mouth of a gigantic cannon. I thought the huge machine moved a little. Maybe it was my imagination. Harvey joined me, and we sat together on what looked like a seat that had been taken out of an airplane.

"Ready!" Harvey called out.

"Take us to Andromeda, Carol," I heard Steve say from far below, and immediately the telescope began to move. The telescope, and Harvey and I with it, swung down and to the side. The chair we were in moved, too. It was on rollers or something, attached to the wall of the round little room. I felt dizzy. Soft light glinted off the curved metal dome like moonlight on rippling water. Then the black of the night sky, pierced with starlight, came into view as we moved toward the slit in the dome. We came to a stop, and I felt a lurch in my stomach, like when I stop on the top of the Ferris wheel and the chair rocks crazily for a second.

"You are there!" Carol called out across the darkness.

"They are where? Where are they?" It was the voice of one of the officers.

"Who are you talking to, Miss?" It was the other one.

"Who *are* you talking to, Carol?" Steve's voice.

"I wish I knew," I heard her say. "Believe me, I wish I knew."

"They're up in the 'scope," Jim yelled. "I can't believe it. They're up there in the 'scope!"

The telescope was more like a tree than I had thought. I had climbed it. It moved like something alive. And it was pretty cozy up here in the "treehouse," now that I was getting used to it. Harvey was peering through an eyepiece in the center of the little circular tub of a room we were perched in. All the while he fiddled with knobs and levers. "What are you doing?" I asked.

"Adjusting . . . adjusting . . . just about got it . . . there!" he said. "Take a look, Casey." Harvey slipped to the side. I looked into the eyepiece.

The frame of sky that I could see was black, a blacker black than I had ever seen before in the night sky in St. Louis. And the black was sprinkled — splattered is more like it in some places — with dozens and dozens, maybe even a hundred or more points of light. They seemed to float in the sky. Some were different colors — yellow, and reddish, and blue, but most were white. And one, off toward the edge, was much bigger and brighter than all the rest.

"Is that Andromeda?" I whispered to Harvey. "The big one near the edge?" The answer seemed obvious.

"No, no, no," he laughed. "Andromeda is big, Casey, but it is not a star. It's a galaxy — many billions of stars. That very bright light you see is one single star, one right near here in the Milky Way. It's only about 600 trillion miles from where we sit. That's why it looks so bright.

"But the rest of the stars you see are in *my* galaxy, Casey. Andromeda. Every one of them is roughly twenty-five thousand times farther away than that bright star here in the Milky Way."

"Oh my liver!" I whispered, and looked some more. "Is this your whole galaxy?"

"Oh your liver, no," Harvey laughed again. "This telescope is very powerful. But *because* it's so powerful it can only see a small section of sky. It covers only a very small part of my galaxy at a time. And your eye can detect only a tiny fraction of the stars that the telescope is pointing at. Right now, for every star you *do* see, there are ten million more looking back at you that you *don't* see."

"Oh my liver, oh my liver, oh my liver." I was panting. When I caught my breath I said, "I don't understand, though. If they're there, why can't I see them?"

"They're too dim, your eye is too weak. Take your pick."

"But stars are bright."

"Indeed they are, but Andromeda is far. Can you see even a very bright light bulb from a thousand miles away?"

"Didn't you say before, though, that Andromeda is close?"

"I said close in the universe, Casey. But the universe is large. Larger than you or I can imagine."

I studied the view some more. Except for the inky blackness and the crisper appearance of the stars, it looked much like what I might see in the sky from my back yard. I had to keep reminding myself that these were *different* stars, in a galaxy far, far away. These were stars I had never seen before, and might never see again.

"Is your star in this part we're looking at?" I asked.

"Yes."

"Which one is it?"

"You cannot see my star," he said, and I could hear affection in his voice. "But it is there, just the same." He smiled at me. "Take a last look," he said. "I think we've troubled these kind people enough."

I looked. And I would always remember.

⇌ Eighteen ⇋

The climb down the ladder didn't seem so hard. We were back on the circular landing before I knew it, starting down the steps to the main floor. The police were still there but they looked pretty much like they had given up. I could hear Carol and Steve talking, and above my head the telescope began to move. They were getting to work.

"I'd like to tell them thanks," Harvey said, pulling me gently toward the work room.

"There he is!" Officer Frank suddenly shouted, and pointed right at Harvey.

Harvey had gone visible again. I suddenly realized I didn't have my spray bottle. In all the excitement I must have put it down somewhere. But where? And, since it was invisible, how was I going to find it?

"Up here! This way!" I shouted to Harvey, and back up the stairs we went. The policemen and Jim were hot on our heels this time. I racked my brain: Where is the spray bottle? What did I do with it?

We reached the landing and kept running, but I saw in a moment that it would do no good. The landing just ran in a big circle around the edge of the dome. It was just a big balcony. Jim was explaining this to the two policemen as they reached the top of the stairs. And now they were splitting up, going in opposite directions. They had us surrounded.

That was when I remembered where the bottle was. I had set it down at the base of the control panel on the main floor. I ran over to the edge of the landing. "Eddie!" I called. "Kathleen!"

"What?!" they called back in unison.

"The spray bottle. I need it for Harvey."

"Where is it?" Eddie called back.

"By the control panel down there."

"How many of them are there?" I heard one of our pursuers say. They were confused. But they were closing in on Harvey and me.

"Look, Casey, over here," Harvey said. He was twenty feet away. And he was holding a door open — a door in the wall of the dome. I hurried over. The doorway opened into a short passage. At the end of it was another door. I opened it. Cold night air swept in. Outside the door was a narrow catwalk, another kind of balcony that went around the observatory. But this one was on the outside, and high off the ground. It would be another trap. But I noticed something else. The door that Harvey had found was mounted in the interior wall of the dome. This second door was mounted in the outside wall. The dome had two "skins." And in between the skins was a hollow space several feet wide and criss-crossed with metal framework, like a jungle gym.

"Harvey, quick! In here." I pointed to the space between the two skins. "Get back in as far as you can so they can't see you."

Harvey did just that, and just in time. When our three pursuers arrived they looked around, unsure where Harvey had gone. "He could get in there," Jim said, pointing to

Harvey's hiding place. This Jim guy was smart. I knew it was time for action.

I threw the outer door open and ran out onto the catwalk. It was about three feet wide. The floor was an open metal grating that clattered when I ran, and there was a steel railing on the outer side. The ground was twenty feet below.

"He's out there!" came a shout from inside.

"I think there's two of 'em," one of the officers said.

"I think there's five," said the other, "ten, maybe."

"I don't care how many there are," Jim said. "Visitor hours are over. They'll have to come back tomorrow, after nine a.m." In a flash he and Officer Fred were out the door after me. I ran, pounding noisily on the steel beneath my feet. They ran after, just a few steps behind.

"I don't see anybody!" Officer Fred shouted. "What's making all the noise? Why can't I see him?"

"He's invisible, remember?"

"Yeah, and my foot's invisible, too," the officer growled. Then, just to make sure, I guess, he looked at his feet.

About halfway around they stopped. I ran a little farther, then I stopped, too. "This is the same thing as inside," Jim said. "This catwalk goes all the way around the dome. And there's only one door. You go the other way. There's no way out this time. This time we'll get him."

The policeman did as instructed. Jim turned in my direction, but he didn't move. He was waiting for me to move first. Soon enough I'd be trapped. I tried to think what to do. Before long I noticed he was moving toward me, slowly, gripping the railing on one side and sliding his hand along the wall on the other. "You should go with the policemen," Jim was saying. "If you want, you can come back tomorrow. Gates open at nine a.m." He was walking funny, sliding his feet from edge to edge of the catwalk as he came along, sweeping for me. He was getting close. "Of course, you're not allowed in the telescope room. You probably know that."

As quickly and as quietly as I could, I pulled off both my shoes. I tapped one shoe on the grating, like a single step. Jim stopped sweeping. He listened. I tapped again, as far as I could reach to my left. He came a quick step forward. I tapped twice and he came two quick steps. He was almost on top of me now. I threw my shoe hard, forward and downward, bouncing it along the catwalk behind me. Then I did the same with my second shoe. It sounded something like running. I flattened myself low and thin against the wall of the observatory dome. Jim flew past.

He was twenty yards past me and still running when I took off in the other direction, back toward the door. I found it and thanked my lucky galaxies when the knob turned and let me in.

I could hear panting and groaning and cursing from somewhere inside the double skin of the dome. Officer Frank was three times as big as Harvey and it wasn't a space built for big people. He wasn't going to catch Harvey in there unless Harvey wanted to be caught.

Still, we had a long way to go to get out of the building and back to the shuttle, St. Louis and, for Harvey, Andromeda. A little invisibility would help. I ran through to the inside landing and called down to Eddie.

"Eddie, have you got it?"

"Absolutely," said Eddie from right behind me.

"Yeow!" I yelled. "Eddie, don't scare me like that. Where's Kathleen?"

"She's guarding the door."

"Okay. Good. Now we've got to find Harvey and get out of here."

"Here I am," said Harvey.

"Yeow! Yeow" Eddie and I yelled together. "Harvey, don't scare us like that," Eddie said.

Harvey was standing right next to us. But we couldn't see him. He was invisible again. "Where'd you come from?" I asked.

"I thought you needed the formula," Eddie said.

"Not you, Eddie. Harvey. Where did *you* come from, Harvey?"

Harvey flashed visible for a few seconds and pointed to an oval shaped opening in the inner skin of the dome wall. It was small, two feet high, and near the floor. It looked like a giant mousehole. I hadn't noticed it before.

"There appear to be several," Harvey said. I scanned right and left and saw two more of the strange holes in the wall. "I can't imagine what they're there for," Harvey mused as he went invisible again. "But it got me out of a tight spot."

We listened to more thumps and groans from Officer Frank between the skins. I had a feeling the mouseholes weren't going to work for him.

"Let's go find Kathleen and get out of here," I said.

"Here I am," Kathleen said, right behind us.

"Yeow! Yeow! Yeow!" Eddie and Harvey and I screamed together.

"Kathleen, don't scare us like that," Harvey complained. He was flicking off and on now, faster.

"What are you doing up here?" I said to Kathleen. "Eddie said you were guarding the door."

"There's nothing to guard. The door's not going to go anywhere. You guys are up here having all the fun."

"Okay. Well, let's get out of here."

We started down the stairs together. Eddie gave Harvey a good spray dousing with the formula, but so far it wasn't doing any good. Harvey was fluttering off and on like a loose light bulb. Carol and Steve were at the bottom of the stairs. Harvey was the only one they could see, sort of, and he was the first to speak.

"Thank you very much for your help," he said.

"Yeah, thanks," I said. "It was . . ." For once words escaped me.

"I take it you found your friend," Steve said.

"All three of them in fact," said Harvey.

"So, you're really from Andromeda?" Carol asked.

"Yes," Harvey said.

"*We're* not from Andromeda," Kathleen said. "We're from St. Louis."

"St. Louis?" Steve said.

"St. Louis County," Eddie explained.

"Lakewood, really," I said. Steve looked more confused than ever. "Earth," I explained.

Carol ran her hand through her hair. "See, Steve, three invisible Lakewoodians and a now-you-see-him, now-you-don't Andromedan. I told you it wasn't an elf."

"One question," Harvey said to Steve and Carol. "If you weren't sure I was from Andromeda, why did you decide to help me?"

"Well, you *said* you were from Andromeda," Carol said. "And I guess I *wanted* you to be from Andromeda."

Steve said, "It just seemed like a good chance to take. I wouldn't get anywhere if I didn't take a chance once in a while."

"Andromedans, either," Harvey said, flashing a static-y grin.

"There he is!" came an excited voice from the top of the stairs. It was the police and Jim, and they were on their way toward us.

⇌ Nineteen ⇋

"You'd best be going," Steve said. "We'll try to slow them down."

We headed for the stairway to the basement level as fast as we could but Harvey was still blinking like a homing beacon. The three men didn't even pause to talk to Carol or Steve.

"Eddie, give me the spray bottle," I heard Kathleen say.

"What for?" Eddie protested.

"Just give it."

"Okay, but there's not much left," Eddie said.

We kept on but our pursuers were gaining. Until, all of a sudden, they stopped. "What was that?" Officer Frank yelled.

"What?" asked Jim.

"My face is all wet. It was like rain or something." He wiped at his face with the heel of his hand. "My hand's wet. Look."

"I don't see anything," Jim said.

"Well, I don't either, but it's wet. Here. Feel it."

"I don't want to. Look! The kid's trespassing after hours. And you're letting him get away."

Jim was right. We were getting away through the clutter of the girders in the basement. Officer Frank was still complaining. "Something sprayed my face, I tell you. Something fishy's going on here."

"Where's Kathleen?" I asked Harvey.

I detect her infrared at the top of the stairs," Harvey said. "She seems to be with our pursuers."

"Hey! Now *I* felt something," yelled Officer Fred. "On my hand. It's wet, just like you said, Frank. Only I can't see anything." There was alarm in his voice.

"Come on, come *on*," Jim urged, starting down.

"I don't know," said Officer Fred. "Something weird's going on."

"I don't want to go down," said Officer Frank.

"Yeah, let's talk this over," Officer Fred said to Jim.

"Kathleen is coming down the steps," Harvey told me. "She's moving toward us."

"Over here," I called in a loud whisper. "Kathleen, we're over here." When she caught up to us I asked, "What did you do?"

"What do you think?" she answered mischievously.

"She sprayed them of course," Eddie said. "Good job, Kathleen. Now, let's get out of here."

We headed for the door and let ourselves out, into the night. "There he goes, he's out the door," Jim called to his companions. I looked back. To my surprise, his buddies were back on the trail again, but they seemed to be moving with a bit more caution.

We kept a steady pace back to the shuttle, the four of us followed by the three of them about fifty yards back. As we drew near to the craft I worried that they would see it. I needn't have though.

"Hey, what the —!" Officer Frank yelled. "Fred, I can't see your hand! What's going on, Freddie? Where's your hand?"

Judging from the sound of the scream, apparently Officer Fred couldn't see his hand either. "Frank, what the . . . FRANK!" he yelled. "Frank, are you okay, man? I can't see your face, or your shoulder or . . . Hey, *your* hand's gone, too!"

"What's going on?" Frank cried out. "What's going on?"

"It's that kid," Jim said.

"And the wet," Officer Fred chimed in. "I told you there was something going on. I told you we shouldn't have kept after him. Now what are we going to do? I can't see my hand," he whined.

"We can't see Frank's face, either," Jim reminded him.

"You know what I think?" Frank said, moving his faceless body up close to Jim. "You want to know what I think, buddy? I'll tell you what I think. I think you should shut UP!"

"Okay," Jim answered meekly.

"You guys wait here for a minute," I said. I walked quietly toward the three men. When I was close, but not too close, I spoke. "It's okay," I said. They jumped and shrieked. "It's okay," I said again when they quieted a little. "I just wanted to tell you. That boy you were chasing. He isn't a boy. And he's not anybody's elf, either. He's a grown-up, and he's not from around here. Ask Carol or Steve. And about your face and your hands. They're okay, too. They're just invisible. They'll come back again in about a day or two. You might flash off and on for a little while. But then I think it'll wear off. At least, it did for me. You might want to lie low for a while."

"Okay," Officer Fred said.

"Maybe I'll take some sick leave," Officer Frank said.

"You're not hurt," I said. "It's just that Harvey has to get home to Andromeda. It's real far and he has to take the wormhole. He wanted to show me where he lives, that's all. And we couldn't afford to get caught." I took a few steps toward the shuttle. Then I stopped and turned back to the three men. They hadn't moved a muscle. "You're not hurt," I said again. "You don't need to worry."

"We won't worry, will we, Frank?" Fred said.

"We'll take sick leave," Frank said again.

"I'll talk to Steve," said Jim.

"Oh, and don't forget about that oil," I said.

"I'll clean it up," Jim said.

"Okay. I'm going now," I said.

"We open again at nine tomorrow," Jim said. "Maybe we'll see you then," he added with a nervous laugh.

"You take it easy," Officer Frank said. "We didn't mean you any harm. No offense."

"No harm done. No offense taken," I said. Then I walked back and joined my friends at the shuttle.

⇌ Twenty ⇋

Palomar Observatory haunted?

By C. A. COLE

The Globe Dispatch

Yesterday evening the famous 200-inch Hale Telescope at Palomar Mountain, California was visited by ghosts, elves, or perhaps aliens from Andromeda Galaxy.

What is definite is that a child of about twelve was found wandering alone in the observatory after closing. Police were summoned.

The boy — an alleged unseen companion proclaimed him a mature adult from another galaxy! — conversed with the observatory staff and demonstrated considerable knowledge in the fields of astronomy and astrophysics, according to a facility spokesperson.

Then the young man vanished into thin air, witnesses say. He and some "invisible" friends — reportedly from

"St. Louis, Earth" — led San Diego County law enforcement officers Frank and Fred (last names were unavailable at press time) and an observatory employee, who wishes to remain anonymous, on a chase throughout the facility. To further confuse matters, a pair of girls' sneakers were found this morning on a catwalk encircling the observatory.

"The officers have taken sick leave and aren't available for comment," said Police Chief Henry. "It's transparent to us that this was all just an early Halloween prank," he said.

But experienced cosmic observers, Carol and Steve, aren't so sure. "He knew his astronomy," Steve assured this reporter. "It's a big, strange universe out there," said Carol.

"Visitors are welcome during normal visiting hours," said the observatory employee who wishes to remain anonymous.

Is Palomar Observatory haunted? Or is it visited by intergalactic aliens?

I took another bite of cereal. Why is it that reporters never even consider the possibility of invisible Earth kids? I thought, as I read the article in the paper Halloween morning. I threw my cereal spoon down in disgust. Good thing Harvey is leaving tonight. They might track him down to Lakewood and then I could imagine the headline: **Palomar mystery solved: Earth invaded by aliens**. I didn't even want to think about how the movie might turn out!

"If I didn't know better, I'd say that the boy in the story sounds like that weird Harvey." Penny was reading over my shoulder.

"Maybe you *don't* know better," I suggested with a smile. Then I decided I'd better get out of there before she figured out what I said. I took the box of cereal upstairs to my bedroom. Kathleen was still asleep. I couldn't see her, just a lump under the covers, but I could hear her snoring. When she woke up, would she be mad that she was still invisible and I wasn't? The magic soap hadn't worked normally at all for Harvey and me. When we got back last night Harvey was visible and me, too. Kathleen and Eddie were not.

"Ow," Eddie said. "You kicked me in the stomach."

"Sorry, Eddie," I said to the invisible kid lying on the floor between the twin beds.

"How come you're not invisible?" he asked. "And does Kathleen snore all the time?"

"No," I lied, "only when she's invisible. Here have some cereal." Eddie crunched and I talked. "I don't know why I'm not invisible. The soap didn't work like normal on Harvey. Of course, he's not only from another planet, he's from another galaxy, too. So he's probably different in some crucial way. And we know that even though he doesn't look it, he's quite old. He even has great grandchildren. But me? I'm not that weird . . ."

"Oh yeah?" Eddie said. I ignored that.

". . . So, maybe because I took that extra flight in the shuttle and used the thigamajigaly to get into the basement of the music store . . ." I sighed. "I don't really know." I hated to admit that, even to myself, much less to Eddie.

"There's something you don't know? You, Casey?" Kathleen said. I hadn't noticed that the snoring had stopped. "Pass that cereal to me. I'm starving. I haven't felt so good in years."

"Is that Kathleen up there or an imposter?" I said. "How can you feel good? You're still invisible. Remember?" I watched the cereal box float in the air for a moment and then get snatched up.

"What do you mean, 'haven't felt so good in years'? You're only eleven," Eddie said. "To hear you talk, you'd think you were twenty-five or something."

"I don't care," she said crunching and talking at the same time. "I had a great time. Remember when you took the shuttle by yourself, Casey, and brought back the magic soap water? And then you and Harvey went up on the telescope?"

"Yeah," I said. "And when you found the bottle, Eddie, and brought it up when I left it down below?"

"And then when you sprayed the soap on those guys, Kathleen?" Eddie said.

"Yeah. We sure did a good job," Kathleen said.

We sure did, I thought. I kind of regretted trying to keep Harvey a secret, trying to use him and the RV to scare Eddie and Kathleen on Halloween. If they hadn't stowed away on the shuttle who knows where Harvey would be today. Scaring Eddie and Kathleen wasn't so important anymore. "Let's go see Harvey," I said. "He's leaving tonight." That was the most important thing: going to see Harvey. Saying goodbye. Saying thanks. Together.

"But first," Kathleen said, "let's go to Uncle Terence and Sophie's and show me off and plan our Halloween party."

"Yeah," Eddie agreed, "a super scary ghost party at the haunted house. Before it takes off for another galaxy."

"You two be the ghosts," I said. "I'll stay visible and help you."

"Yes!" they both said. Sheets and blankets flew through the air.

⇌ Twenty-one ⇋

Uncle Terence and Sophie didn't answer their door. Dr. Poof and Madame Farsight, the people who invented the magic soap, did. But something strange was going on. Dr. Poof looked much shorter than I remembered. His purple, red and orange carnival pants were rolled up at the ankles. Madame Farsight looked different in some way, too, even though she was wearing her usual bright, colored skirt and had the purple ribbon around her short curly wig. I hadn't seen the Spellings — their real name — since the summer, when they left town with their little boy, Kevin.

"Where's Kevin?" I asked. A look passed between them, an Uncle Terence and Sophie kind of look. They took off their wigs. Uncle Terence and Sophie were dressed in the Spellings' carnival outfits! "We didn't know what to go as until I found the clothes the Spellings left behind," Uncle Terence said.

"Surprise," Kathleen said. "I'm invisible."

"Me, too," said Eddie.

"Everybody's dressed for Halloween except for you, Casey, and you, Bumps," Sophie said. "We'll have to do something about that."

While eating an orange and black dinner of cheese pizza with black olives, we told Sophie and Uncle Terence about the exciting adventures of the night before. And when we were done we started working on our costumes.

Sophie dressed me up all in black, with ears, a nose, whiskers, and a tail, and then pronounced me a cat. "Just like Camomile," she said. Cam meowed. I meowed. Bumps barked happily, and decided to remain a dog.

At dusk we left Sophie and Uncle Terence's and headed for Harvey's. We decided to walk. All along the way Eddie and Kathleen made eerie, ghostly noises. Grotesquely carved, candle-lit pumpkins gaped from windows and porches along our route; ghouls and goblins roamed the streets; tiny cloth ghosts hovered among the trees; and in one yard a mummy sat up in an old wooden coffin.

But it wasn't until we got to the cemetery and walked the dark path through the woods that I really got spooked. Wind whistled in the trees, and leaves swirled thickly to the ground. Harvey's house was silent and dark. Shockingly silent and dark. A sudden wind came up and a shutter banged loudly against an upstairs window. Back and forth it swung. Steadily. Loudly. Uncle Terence knocked on the door. When he took hold of it, the door fell into his hands, rotten at the hinges.

"Harvey?" Sophie called at the door. There was no answer. We stepped inside. Uncle Terence played the flashlight around the room. Cobwebs. Nothing else.

Maybe this *wasn't* a spaceship from another galaxy. Maybe it *wasn't* an intergalactic RV. Maybe that *wasn't* a shuttle craft perched at one corner of a ship. Maybe it was just an old, run down house with a tower. Maybe I had dreamed the whole thing.

"I don't understand," I said to everybody and to nobody in particular. "Harvey said he has to leave tonight. Where is he?" Could I have imagined the whole amazing story?

"Maybe he's packing," Kathleen suggested.

"Or asleep," Sophie said.

"Maybe he's in the bathroom," Eddie said. "Of course, being from another galaxy and all it's entirely possible that he has a whole other . . . you know . . . situation." Eddie was too disgusting. I took mental aim, then swung my arm out, cutting an arc backwards through the air to my right. "Oomph," Eddie gasped.

"But where *is* Harvey?" I said again. "Why isn't he here?"

A figure appeared at the top of the stairs. It held a candle. Shadows and candlelight flickered across the not-quite-familiar face. Is that Harvey? I wondered. Cam meowed and ran up the stairs. Bumps stayed by me.

"I apologize for not answering the door," the figure said. It *was* Harvey, but he sounded different. Heavy, and tired. Maybe sad.

"What's the matter, Harvey?" I asked.

"I have a bit of a problem, I'm afraid," he said.

"What kind of a problem?" Uncle Terence asked.

"Maybe we could help," Eddie said.

"It's very kind of you to offer," Harvey said. "And, yes, perhaps you could. But, you see, that's part of the problem."

"Being part of the solution is being part of the problem?" I asked.

"I'm afraid so."

"Will someone please explain what we're talking about?" Kathleen said.

"Perhaps that would be a good idea, Harvey," Sophie said gently.

Harvey came down the stairs and sat on the last step. He rubbed his hands together, twisting them over and through one another like you do under the dryers that blow air in restrooms. "Well," he began, "it seems I have a valve problem."

"An *induction* valve problem?" I asked.

"A prodibulator induction valve problem," Harvey said.

"A *central* prodibulator induction valve *obstruction*?" I said.

"Precisely," Harvey said. "I've explained to Casey that I've had to manually synchronize the peripheral dopulator production system every few hours since my arrival on Earth."

"You said it wasn't hard, though," I reminded him.

"It isn't, but it is basic maintenance. It has to be done on time," Harvey said, "and without fail. Miss even one synchronization and the induction valve is almost certain to become obstructed."

"And you missed one on the trip to Mount Palomar I'll bet," Eddie said. "The trip took longer than you planned."

"I was enjoying myself so much that —"

"You miscalculated," Eddie said.

"— I, basically, forgot," Harvey said.

"And so now the valve is screwed up."

"Precisely, Eddie," Harvey said, wringing his hands again. "It's screwed up."

"But tonight's your one chance!" Kathleen said. "If the valve is obstructed you can't get home!"

"Precisely," Harvey said again.

"Perhaps we could help you clear the valve?" Uncle Terence asked.

"Precisely." This time it was Eddie who spoke, and there was authority in his voice. "Yeah, we'll *un*-obstruct it. And then we'll synchronize it, and prodibulate it, and whatever else it needs. And that'll be that and you can be on your way." He brushed his hands together with satisfaction, as though the job were already completed. But Harvey didn't look as pleased.

"It's not so easy as that, my friend," Harvey said.

"Why not?" Eddie wanted to know. "If synchronizing isn't hard, unplugging a valve should be a cinch."

"Unfortunately, this time you are quite incorrect," Harvey said. "You see, synchronization can be done easily by one person. Valve clearance, on the other hand, is a delicate operation. It requires nine people who are —"

"There's nine of *us*!" I exclaimed victoriously.

"— trained and experienced at working as a team," Harvey finished.

"There are only six of us, dear," Sophie corrected.

"I was counting Bumps and Camomile," I said, then felt silly for it.

"That still only makes eight," Sophie said. "And much as we love them, Casey, and they love us, I don't think we can count on Camomile or Bumps this time." She looked at the child-like figure on the steps, then asked hopefully and in a way that made me feel better, "Can we, Harvey?"

Harvey shook his head. And for a long while, nobody said anything.

"But we are a team," Kathleen said, almost to herself. "That's a start."

"I don't think it's in quite the same way Harvey means," Uncle Terence said. "Besides, as Sophie pointed out, we're only six."

"And we're not trained," Eddie said.

"Perhaps Harvey could train us," Sophie suggested.

"Maybe," Uncle Terence said, "but we're *still* only six."

"Some of us could do double duty," I said. "I could."

"So could I," Kathleen said.

"Me, too," Eddie said.

"So there it is. A soon-to-be-trained team of nine!" I was actually smiling.

"Just one problem," Harvey said. "It's dangerous. I realized I was probably going to have a valve problem on the way back from Palomar. But it's too dangerous. That's why I haven't asked you."

"Well, what's the worst that could happen?" Eddie said.

"We only have one chance to clear the valve. If the timing isn't perfect, I'll be here forever. Worse yet, all of you might slip into the wormhole with me."

"So? We have a cool trip to Andromeda. Then you send us back. Like one of those tubes at the drive-up at the bank." Eddie made a sucking sound to symbolize the thirty million trillion mile round trip through the wormhole. "Cool," he said again.

"It's not as simple as that," Harvey said.

"Why not?"

"Because a wormhole is not a vacuum tube at the bank, Eddie. There's no telling if you could return. Ever."

"Oh," Eddie said in a voice that I could barely hear.

⇌ Twenty-two ⇋

Everyone was quiet again. We just stood there, and all the while I could feel the time being pulled away, like sand beneath our feet on an ocean beach. I pushed the little light button on my watch. "Look," I said, "there's less than five hours left before midnight. If we don't do something, you'll be stuck here forever. Your family and friends will never see you again. You'll never see *them* again." I waited a moment, but still nobody responded. "You said it was too dangerous, and that's why you couldn't ask us for help. But what if we volunteer to help? That would be different, wouldn't it?"

"I couldn't ask you to risk it."

"And you're not asking. I'm offering. It's the Second Rule of the Universe," I said: "Help out when you can."

"I'm in," said Eddie.

"Me, too," Kathleen said.

Harvey looked at Sophie and Uncle Terence. Each of them, in turn, nodded and smiled as his eyes met theirs.

"Besides," I said, "Kathleen is right. We're a good team. I figure we'll do it right. The first time."

"You are very good friends," he said quietly. "Now, listen carefully to what I tell you."

Harvey lined us up in front of the control panel. He was first, then Sophie, Uncle Terence, and me. Eddie and Kathleen were numbers five and six, because they were invisible and couldn't do double duty even though they'd volunteered. "Too risky," Harvey said. "You might trip or something as you move to your new positions." Double duty was left to Sophie, Uncle Terence, and me. Then he had us hold hands. He said it would increase the molecular communication between us, and that was good, because timing and teamwork were everything. "Besides," he added, "the touch of a friend lends courage."

At first it appeared that valve clearance wasn't so difficult. The actual clearance maneuvers were simple enough to learn: just pushing buttons and pulling levers and turning dials. But getting the timing right wasn't so easy. We stood in front of the control panel for over three hours and practiced our routine — never touching the controls, of course — dozens of times. Holding hands helped, but we had to know when to let go, too. Sophie had the first double duty and she was nervous about it. And once Uncle Terence pulled my lever instead of turning his dial. And three times I plowed into invisible Eddie during my move from position #4 to position #9. The third time was the worst: I collided with Eddie who fell into Kathleen who grabbed Sophie for support and she tumbled into Uncle Terence. I could tell Harvey was having second thoughts about his team: his only hope for getting back to Andromeda.

We kept on practicing. When the 53rd - 61st attempts went without a hitch Harvey decided we should rest for a few minutes before it would be time for the real thing.

"There will be a 63.472 second delay," he reminded us one last time, "between the entry of the final coordinates and my departure." Harvey looked directly at me. Entry of the coordinates was the ninth and final job. *My* job. "During that time all of you *must* vacate the ship or you will be taken into the wormhole with it. We must say our goodbyes now as there will be no time once we start the clearance procedure. Remember," he warned, "get clear of the ship. You will have no second chance."

We all said goodbye to Harvey then. "I couldn't have had a better vacation, Casey," he told me. He went on to the others, and I thought about the stars I saw last night — Andromeda stars — and especially about Harvey's star, that I didn't see; I thought about that ant on the giant-sized piece of paper, looking for a shortcut home; and I thought about the Celts, and their belief that Halloween was the time when the walls between worlds are thinnest. I didn't know if they were right or not. But I knew the wormhole would disappear when this day ended. I knew they were right *this* Halloween.

We took our positions one last time. We waited. A digital countdown clock raced towards zero. At the precise instant it reached that number Harvey pulled a lever. Clearance was underway.

Sophie dropped Harvey's hand. He quickly set about checking final adjustments at the control panel, making certain that everything would be ready for wormhole passage once the obstruction was cleared. Sophie pushed the glowing button in front of her, let go of Uncle Terence with her other hand, then headed for position #7. Meanwhile, Uncle Terence turned his dial smoothly and confidently to the assigned value, squeezed my hand lightly and let go, heading for #8. The instant Uncle Terence's fingers left mine I reached for the long-handled lever above my head. Slowly and steadily I pulled it down to the red line, paused, then just as slowly and steadily pushed it back to its starting place. I released Eddie's hand, took two steps straight backwards to make sure there would be no collision with him and started toward my #9 position. Eddie's job was an almost instant button-push. He was done, just like he was supposed to be, before I'd finished backing up.

Kathleen's job at station #6 required a five second delay after Eddie was finished. Then she had to do it again after Sophie and after Uncle Terence. Exactly a five second delay each time. I could hear her whispering the numbers, and the slow, rhythmic tapping of Eddie's foot helping her to keep the pace. As I passed I saw her #6 knob slide, as if by magic, from right to left and the pressure indicator above begin to rise. Just as we'd practiced. Suddenly Sophie's left hand was freed at position #7. She turned a dial. At the same time I moved into my new position, taking Uncle Terence's waiting hand just as he and Sophie let go on his left and Kathleen did her delay move. Then Uncle Terence reached up and flipped a toggle switch as though it were no more consequential than turning on the television. Kathleen did her delay maneuver the third and final time. Now it was up to me.

My last job was a two-handed one. Both locator coordinates had to be entered simultaneously. I let go of Uncle Terence's hand for the second time, took a deep breath to steady myself, and reached toward the two dials, glowing orange in front of me. Slowly I turned the knobs, watching the readings flash in the little screen above each dial, changing in a constant blur. As I neared the values I was looking for I slowed. And when the exact numbers appeared in the screens I released the knobs and jumped back, as though I had found myself holding two hairy spiders. I fell down.

Immediately a digital clock showed 63.472 and began rushing down towards zero, reeling the numbers off in thousandths of a second. I was hypnotized by the clock and couldn't move, but the spell was broken by Bumps' tongue on my face and by ten hands pulling me off the floor. By the time I regained my feet the clock was at 59. I looked at Harvey. We all did.

"Thank you," he said, and I thought I saw a tear glisten in his eye. Then he spoke his final words to us, with a loving sternness that could not be disobeyed. "Go," he said. "Now!"

We took hold of one another's hands again, as we'd practiced, so that no one could get lost or left behind. We started down the first stairs as the clock cascaded past 53 seconds, Bumps and Camomile leading the retreat.

It was a reckless descent at the second staircase, with more than one fall and bruise along the way. But we reached the main floor in one piece. We sprinted in a long chain across the empty main floor, and were out the door hardly a second later. We were running as we hit the dirt in front of the rickety steps of the "house" and were still running into the trees when Uncle Terence stopped us. "We're clear," he panted. "We're okay."

We turned. The house was there, quiet and spooky as ever. A faint glow leaked from the tower control room, and in its dim light I saw silhouetted a small figure. He raised one hand in farewell.

I raised mine in return. We all did, even Eddie and Kathleen, who were blinking on and off. Looking back on it, what I did next was odd. I knew the time was about up and, instinctively, I braced myself for the huge spaceship's departure. I waited for the engines to ignite and the ground to shake, and I covered my ears to protect them from the deafening roar. But, of course, it didn't happen like that.

One moment I was looking at Harvey. The next moment he and his ship were gone.

⇌ Twenty-three ⇋

We walked quietly along the path towards the edge of the woods and our homes. It was Eddie who broke the silence.

"No one will believe us, you know."

"You were planning to *tell*?" Kathleen said.

"Look up there," I said, pointing to the spot in the sky Harvey had shown me from the tower window. The trees still held some leaves and blocked the glare from the few streetlights in our neighborhood. "I'll bet Harvey's home already."

"It might have been fun to go with him," Kathleen said.

"Perhaps," Uncle Terence answered.

"No one will believe us," Eddie said again. "Not in a kazillion years."

"Don't be so sure," Sophie said. "Some people will believe anything. Even true things."

I was pretty sure I could see it, the smudge of light in the sky that contained more than a hundred billion stars. And my friend Harvey.

ABOUT THE AUTHORS

Terry and Wayne Baltz were born and raised in St. Louis, although at the time they were better known as Terry Swekosky and Wayne Baltz. They now live in Colorado, where they divide their time between living in the city (with the luxury of indoor plumbing) and living in their one-room cabin in the mountains (with the luxuries of far views, deer and elk, bunnies, badgers, mountain bluebirds, coyotes, eagles, and a pretty nice view of Andromeda).

The authors regularly visit elementary and middle schools where they talk with children about writing, creative expression, and the publishing process. You may contact them at the publisher's address, by telephone (970/493-6593), or at http://www.pageplus.com/baltz